Tainted LOVE

LIVELL JAMES

TAINTED LOVE

Copyright © 2019, Livell James

First electronic publication: May 2019

This is a work of fiction. Names, character, places and incidents are products of the writer's imagination or have been used fictitiously and are not to be construed as real. Any resemblance to person, living or dead, actual events, locale or organizations is entirely coincidental. The author does not have any control over and does not assume any responsibility for third party websites or their content.

Published in the United States of America

Editing – Amy Harris and Grace Brennan

Photograph – Randy Sewell: RLS Model Images Photography

Cover Model – Jake Reeves

Cover Designer – Tammie Smith: Renegade Covers

Formatting: Dark Water Covers & Formatting

For all of you that believe in me and continue to support my journey as an author.
My beautiful wife for not killing me and kicking me out of the house during the writing and editing process.

In memory of my amazing son Alec
July 30, 1998 - August 18, 2016

Chapter 1
AUSTIN

I've spent the last thirty minutes in my car, sitting on my hands to keep them from freezing, but that idea doesn't work when it's this damn cold. I just hoped my heat would kick in soon.

I'm sure you're all thinking, "Why would he be sitting in his car when he could have waited in the house for it to warm up?"

That's where the story begins. I don't have a home. Yup, you read it right, I'm homeless—but not helpless.

I was allowed to sleep at the shelter last night as the temperature was well below freezing. That's not something that often happens here in the southern states. They usually wouldn't give two shits about a young guy like me who has a job. Yes, I have a job, but I only work a few days a week. I somehow convinced them that it wasn't a good idea for me to sleep in my car. I might be making assumptions, but I'm almost sure they would never make anyone sleep in their car if they have space for them in the shelter. However, here I sit in my car, freezing my ass off.

So why am I homeless, you ask?

Both of my folks were killed in a car accident about a month ago, and they had nothing they could call their own. The cause of the crash was never found—at least that's what they tell me. All I know is that they ran off the road and ended up going over a cliff. The more I think about it, the harder it is for me to believe they just suddenly left the road for no damn reason at all. However, you can only take the word of the person who wrote the report.

The house we lived in was a month-to-month rental home. I couldn't afford to keep the house on my four hundred dollars a month job. We'd only moved here about a year ago, so I didn't have anyone I knew well enough to help me out. None of the family on my mom's side would take me in because I was "the bad child." Truth be told, they just didn't like the idea of Mom and Dad being together. Even after twenty-something years, her family still hated my dad.

Why? They were assholes and judged him on the color of his skin. Her family also never let Dad live down the fact that he'd gotten into some trouble when he was younger. They all thought if they took me in that I would follow suit. As far as my dad's side of the family, he had none left. He was raised by a single mother, and until the day she died, he still didn't know who his dad was. Grandma died before I was born.

Yes, I know my tale is starting out as a huge sob story. Let's all feel sorry for the twenty-year-old homeless guy.

Well, this is not how it was meant to be.

I work at Jones', a family owned grocery store, on Tuesday and Thursday, helping unload the trucks and put away stock. There isn't a lot of storage space downtown in a city like Shreveport, Louisiana, so they order merchandise according to sales. The store is more of a neighborhood market than a regular grocery store; Just a small butcher shop, a few aisles across the middle store, and a couple of cashier spaces at the front. The produce is mostly local.

This was the first job I was offered after my parents were killed. I'm still looking for a full-time position. I know there has to be something more for me out there somewhere. Besides, who wants to say they are homeless at my age?

Before all of this, I had plans to go to Louisiana State, but now, here I sit, in this cold ass, beat up silver 2008 Nissan Versa. My future is playing out a lot differently than I thought it would.

Some of the ice has cleared from my windshield from blasting the defroster and me scraping away at it. Now that I can see enough, I put the car in drive. I peer over the steering wheel, gripping it as if it's going to fall out of my hands. Off to work I go.

This weather has been so weird lately, in typical southern fashion. It was seventy degrees a few days ago and now it's freezing. The sky is grey and looks like winter will be setting in for a while. The streets are all dark and slick from the dew freezing on them the night before. I truly need some sunshine in my life, but that will have to come another day.

Just like any other work day, I pull the car around the back side of the old brick building where employees park. This is also where I sleep in my car ninety nine percent of the time. The building is at the end of a strip of shops that line a one-way street. The grocery store is very recognizable, painted a brick red color on the front and down the side facing the street, with a huge city mural painted in the center. It sits on the outer edges of downtown, and was shadowed by the enormous skyscrapers surrounding it.

Pulling into the lot, I see something—some*one*—out of the corner of my eye. It's a beautiful female who looks to be about twenty-years-old or so, standing in the middle of the spot where I usually park. She's rather tall, with a slender build, ice-cold blue eyes that I notice as I get closer, and long blonde hair flowing to one side under the black hoodie she has pulled over her head.

I turn into the space on the other side, facing the back of another building. It was very odd to see some random girl just standing in my parking space. She's never been around here any time before today, so I just decided not to push her from the space and take one on the other side. By the time I parked the car and grabbed my apron from the floorboard, she was gone. It was as if she had never been there. I know I saw her! She'd been there clear as day, and as beautiful as she was, she had to be real. There was no way the cold weather was getting to my brain to that extent, and there was no way my mind conjured up a woman that gorgeous. It just wasn't possible.

I stand still, just staring, and then start turning in circles while I try to figure out where she'd run off to. Just as I make my way to the back of the building, I'm almost hit by the old screen door in the back of the market, the door cracking and popping as it opens, Mr. Jones almost running me over.

"Well good morning to you too, young man! Just run over my ass next time," he said as he shuffled off to take the garbage he was carrying to the dumpster.

I'm not sure how I was running over him when he almost knocked my ass down with the door, and I just stand there looking like a dumbass.

"Hey Mr. Jones, did you see a pretty little lady hanging around outside this morning?" I asked.

"No, I ain't seen anyone or anything other than this damn trash all morning. You kids really need to start cleaning up around here more," he rumbles in his thick southern accent.

"Now, you know I only work two days a week, Sir," I said as I hurried to get away from him.

Mr. Jones is in his seventies, at least, and has had the store for about forty years. His father owned it before him and so forth. His son, Adam, pretty much manages the place and will soon take it over if old man Jones ever retires. The family has been trying to talk him into it for years. I will most likely be the same way when I'm his age. The store keeps him going, even if he is salty all the damn time. Once I make it into the stock room, I'm able to clock in and head out on the floor to put out stock.

HALEY

Those damn voices have been taunting me for days.

I haven't been sleeping well at all lately with these voices in my head. I've known I was a medium all my life. For much of that time, I refused to admit it or even answer the spirits that taunt me in my sleep. However, it was different this time. They weren't giving up.

"Austin! You must find Austin, he needs your help," was all I heard over and over in my head for hours on end.

Waking myself up and dragging my ass to the bathroom, I look in the mirror and see the huge bags sagging under my bloodshot eyes. I managed to get a shower and put on my black sweater with the hood on it, gloves, and knee-high socks to keep my legs warm. I apply just enough makeup to make my eyes not look so bad: eye shadow, liner, and mascara. Thanks to my mother, who gave me my ice blue eyes, they always standout when I put liner on them. Not that I don't stand out anyway, I'm a slender female at almost six feet tall. If I dare wear heels, I stand over six feet.

Today is one of the coldest days we've seen in the south in a few years. Today is also the day I decided to listen to this couple who've been pretty much begging me to find their son. I live in a town just outside of Shreveport Louisiana, called Greenwood. My parents moved me here a few years ago, into an apartment to try to keep me safe from all the spirits and many other paranormal things that went on in the city. They asked me not to come back there because it wasn't safe for me. I'm still not sure how and why it isn't safe for me because my brother Jonah still lives there with them. Shouldn't it be just as unsafe for him?

I'll probably never know the reasons why. For now, I must make my way out into this nasty cold weather. Walking out my front door, I throw my hood over my head.

"Fuck." I almost slipped on the ice going down the steps.

Making my way to the car, I start slinging curses as I see I have to try to scrape ice from my windshield. Digging in my purse, I finally found my old debit card and do my best to remove the ice. Finally getting enough that I can see from the driver's side of the car, I turn on the defrost and sit for what seems like hours, listening to "Tainted Love" as the song plays on the radio.

I put the address that the voices gave me into my cell phone's GPS as I was waking up this morning, then proceeded to back out of my driveway. The GPS informed me the destination was eighteen miles away. I knew it was downtown and had already prepared myself with my head-phones. Playing loud music helps me avoid the other spirits while driving through town. Today, I was going to find this guy who I only know as Austin.

After my short drive, I finally make it into downtown.

Shreveport is a mixture of old and new. The streets are lined with old buildings among the backdrop of skyscrapers along the Red River. It's seated in Caddo Parish with a popu-lation of just over two hundred thousand people. A few casinos dot the landscape along the river banks.

Many would be scared shitless if they knew the things that happened here after dark—or in broad daylight, for that matter.

At last, I find the address. The place is a market with just a few spots to park out front.

"Why am I here?" I wondered aloud.

With nowhere to park, I decided to drive down the street to the next available spot I could find. I only just noticed that it was almost three blocks from my car, as I walked back to the address I was given. When I reached the building, a large painting suddenly grabbed my attention. I was entranced to the point I just stared at artwork for at least ten minutes. I was there for so long that it took me a while to realize I walked along the side of the building to the backside where there was a parking lot with at least ten spaces!

"*Damn it!*" I cursed under my cold breath.

This would have kept me from walking so far in the brutally frigid weather! I pulled my hood even tighter to avoid exposing my ears and pushed my hair over my left side on the shoulder. After standing in one spot for a few minutes, I noticed I was in the middle of one of the parking spaces when a silver Nissan came rushing into the lot. I froze for a moment and waited for the guy to park. As soon as I saw he'd looked down to unbuckle his seatbelt, I jetted my way back around the building, hoping I wasn't noticed. Because I'm sure I was just standing there, staring off into space. He had to think I was crazy as hell if he'd seen me.

I have to find this Austin guy, and I was on a mission.

Making my way around the building, I brush myself off and walk inside the front door. I then realized I forgot my headphones when I start hearing voices. I am thankful I have learned to block them out when I need to. The exceptions are such as the parents of this guy when they attach themselves to me.

The store is a quaint little place with a few young girls at the front checkout and the cute small produce market off to the side of the store. As I walked past the cashiers, I noticed one of them is someone I know. I try to avoid contact with her until I find the person I'm looking for, but I may stop to speak to her on my way out.

I see the butcher shop and a guy standing just outside the door that must lead to the stock room in the back. The first thing I noticed was his beautiful olive skin. As I got closer, I could see his amazing eyes, and his arms look well defined. His broad chest caught my attention moments later in the way his tight tee shirt left nothing to the imagination. This had to be the guy I was looking for. The voices told me his features were striking, just like those of his dad.

His shiny hair shaved on the side, with curls piled on the top, and his strong jawline tells me this is for sure the guy I am looking for. It has to be. Bracing myself, I approach him.

"Hi, I'm looking for Austin."

He looked at me as if I broke his arm or something, and he appeared ready to run at any second.

I heard a whisper from a faint female voice. "Protect him."

Chapter 3
AUSTIN

Oh shit!

That's the chick I saw outside walking towards me. As my eyes met hers, a shiver ran up my spine, telling something wasn't quite right about her. My first instinct was to run into the stock room as fast as I could, but I was stuck in place, and my feet felt as if they weighed hundreds of pounds.

Her gaze had me equally frozen as the cold blue in her eyes. The closer she gets to me, the more I feel my heart start to race. Then she spoke.

"I'm looking for Austin," she said in the most angelic voice I think I have ever heard.

Why the hell is this stunningly beautiful woman looking for me? Did I win the damn lottery, and someone forgot to tell me? I try to speak but my words came out as a mumble.

"What, um-mm, what did Austin do?" was all I could say once I shook the stupid look from my face.

"Protect him," she said, staring at me dead in the eyes as if she had spaced out and forgotten where she was.

"What do you mean, protect him?" I asked, trying not to yell as I spoke.

"Damn voices always talking to me..." she started to mutter before pausing, trying to get back on task. She cleared her throat.

"Hi, I'm looking for Austin."

"Who said I was Austin?" As she reached out her hand to shake mine, I can tell she is nervous, and something's weighing on her mind. "Are you okay? I think you must have slipped on the ice or something this morning and hit your head. Because I do not hear any voices, other than the couple at the butcher counter over there." I pointed my finger in the direction of meat department.

Once I notice that my face had a perma-grin, I shake my head and repeated without the mumble this time.

"Why are you looking for Austin?"

"Your parents sent me!" she suddenly blurted out.

My mouth dropped open. I must have looked like I was in pain because I could feel my face tighten and my eyes pop out.

"You must have me mistaken for another Austin, lady."

"Austin, you have to believe me. I know it sounds crazy, but you must listen. They are speaking to me," Haley replied, raising her voice.

"My parents are dead! I don't need some weird ass pretty blonde rushing in on me while I'm at work. It sounds pretty damn crazy to me that you say you knew my folks and are talking to them."

"They say you are in danger," she says before I cut her off.

"Now if you will excuse me, I have to get back to work." Thankfully, I'm standing right next to the door. I roll my eyes and turn to walk away from her.

I walk into the stockroom as fast as I can, trying not to call attention from anyone else in the store. I closed myself into the meat cutting room as my chest began to tighten, sitting on the stock cart and trying to catch my breath. How the hell could she know my parents, and how did she know where to find me? Talking to them? How is that even possible? Can people have actual conversations with dead people?

I have to get out of this room before I'm seen and get in trouble for goofing off. It's been about fifteen minutes and, surely, she's gone by now. I stand from where I am sitting, lean against the wall, and whip off my apron that has the market's logo in the middle of my chest. I make sure it isn't wrinkled before walking out on the sales floor again, since it had just been balled up in my hand for the past fifteen minutes. Still a little shaken, I eased my head outside the door to see if she was still standing there.

Not seeing her, I pushed past the door, leaving it swinging behind me as I speed walk toward the front of the store. I see one of the cashiers, Stacy, standing with her ass leaning on the counter, twirling her hair with her index finger. I suppose this is what they do when they are bored at work.

She is about five-foot-tall, red hair, sparkly blue eyes, and has freckles dusting her face. She has that cute girl next door look about her. Stacy works here five days a week, but she never talks much.

"Stacy, did you see the blonde chick in the hoodie? Did she leave?" I ask.

Stacy had a crazy, almost fearful look in her eyes when she sees me.

"She left her number and said you really need to call her. She left walking up the street a few minutes ago. She said you're in danger!"

"She's a nut case! Why am I in danger? I hardly know anyone in this town, other than the few friends I made when we moved here a few years ago," I answered reasonably.

"Austin, I would not blow this off as if it were nothing. Why would she come to your job if there wasn't some truth to what she says?" Stacy argued.

"She came to my job because no one knows where I may be sleeping in my car on any night of the week," I pointed out.

I put the paper Stacy handed me with the number on it in my pocket and try to get back to work. I can't focus on anything. All I can do is think about my parents. I wonder, even if this were true, why would they send some chick to tell me I am in danger? Maybe I should have given her more time to explain before running off to the meat room like a scared child. Perhaps she is telling the truth, and she's one of those people who communicates with the spirits or dead people. Whatever, that shit still freaks me out.

Chapter 4
HALEY

What a fucking prick! I walked three damn blocks in the cold to help this guy, and I get a door slammed in my face. He has to know the truth, but I shouldn't be the one having to tell him. Why did his parents come to me from the afterlife, knowing who my parents are, and the world in which I come from? There have to be other mediums in this city.

Hopefully, Stacy doesn't rat me out. I had no idea someone from our coven would be working in the store with Austin. It's more surprising that I ran into Stacy, since not many of us are out and about in the daytime hours. Those of us that do are called daywalkers.

I'm the only medium born to my family. Our part of the city is hidden to the human eye, right in the middle Shreveport. We have to enter through secret passages placed throughout the city. I wouldn't call it underground—okay, so maybe it *is* underground, but we like to think of it as our own town. This town is made of vampires and the lucky human slaves in which they feed upon.

These humans come to the city willingly. They've all been sworn to secrecy to never let outsiders know where the passages are located, and will be executed if the bonds are broken. This really doesn't matter, since our city isn't visible to human sight unless they have drunk from the wrist of a vampire. It is then and only then that they can they see the logos placed on the openings leading into the passages. Humans only come into the underground by way of the vampire.

My parents chose to let me live among the humans in the outside world, as I was one of the lucky ones to be a daywalker. They said it was to protect me, once again. We're not the only vampires that walk the city at night, but even so, I haven't quite figured out what my parents are protecting me from yet. Because how is moving me away from the coven helping me stay protected?

And on top of that, now I'm supposed to protect someone else?

Speaking of which, I need to find my parents and figure out what I should to do about this one. I find a bench to sit on for a bit while I collect my thoughts.

Wait, I remember this place.... I've been here before with my parents when I was younger. I remember they took me through a passage somewhere around here. I can hear my mom's voice in my head as I stand up and look around.

"Where the triangle meets the road, then, there we must go."

She always tried to make our adventures outside of the dark chambers we lived in under the city more of a fairytale. Mom had a weird nursery rhyme way of explaining where we were going. So here I stand on a busy ass street, looking for this damn triangle. I know where other passages are, but I'm here so I shall find it.

There are a lot of shops, bars, and restaurants lining the street. The smell of burnt grease is making me sick to my stomach. I'm very unusual in that, along with my powers as a medium, I wasn't born with the craving for blood. My mother is human, and my father is a vampire. Yes, I am a dhampir and will remain human until my death, upon which I will become a vampire. Ninety percent of us daywalkers were born of human and vampire parents. We are needed to let others know what happens in the world outside during the day.

And the voices are back!

"You must hurry! Our son is in grave danger. You have to make him believe you!"

I shake my head as the smell of gas from the passing cars and fried foods enveloped my nose.

"*Okay*! You two have to stop randomly yelling in my ear about your son! I have to figure out where I am going and what the hell I am doing before I can help your son!"

I didn't notice that I had been looking down at the ground as I walked until just then. I raise my head to look up at the street, and there it was! The triangle was staring me right in the face. Two buildings where the roads forked give the illusion of a triangle dipping into the street. Now I just have to figure out where this passage is supposed to be. Maybe once I get there, I'll remember.

It feels like I have walked two miles already when I finally get to where the triangle meets the road, and I see an adult bookstore with our coven's decal on the door. Yes, we have a coven sticker, shown only to members as to where our passageways are located, as I said before. It's not like we go around wearing that shit. However, I don't remember going into the adult bookstore when I was younger. Oh well, screw it. Here goes nothing.

Most of the time, the people who own and run the stores where we cross over into our area of the city are part of our coven. They may also have been partners to someone in our coven as well. This business must have changed from the headshop I remember it being as a child. I push the door open, and my eyes are filled with lingerie, adult movies, and whatever else lies inside these places. Loud dance music is playing on the speakers in the ceiling.

I see a chick, who I suppose works here, sitting on the front counter. She is twisting her hair around her finger, smacking on gum, and dazing off into space. Her jet-black hair is pulled up into pigtails, and she is wearing fishnet stockings with a bustier and schoolgirl skirt.

"Excuse me. I'm looking for the passage," I say as I walk up behind her.

The clerk jumps as if I were a ghost or some shit. I mean, I know I am as pale as one, but damn...

"You're looking for what passage? I have no idea what this is you speak of."

The girl turns and will not look me in the eyes. Then she decides she is going to try to ignore me standing here.

I grab her by the right arm, and extend my fangs.

Why the hell did I get my dad's fangs? Yes, I have fucking fangs. While they are of no use to me, they are effective at scaring the hell out of people. So, while I have them on display, I show them and raise my voice. "My father is Angelus DeVile, and I will have him here in less than two minutes! Now I suggest you show me where the passage is!"

I can't explain the look she has on her face after I finally release her arm from my grip. She shakes her head and tells me to follow her. I look over my shoulder to make sure no one is watching before she leads me into this room behind the crushed red velvet curtains. She pulls the curtain open and lets me walk into the room without her. She stays outside the door, holding the curtain and staring at me as if I have lost my damn mind.

The room looks more like a stripper lounge and is entirely out of place. I ask no questions about the room and just hope that I'm out of here soon. I have to make sure not to come back this way upon returning to my car. Surely there has to be another way, someplace near where I parked beside here.

She points to a shelf on the back wall of the room and tells me to remove the purple book before she runs back to the front of the store as if she feared something may jump out at her. I pull the book from the shelf, and there is a latch behind it. I grab ahold of it and pull it down releasing, a small door from the wall to the left of the shelf. This is nothing like I remembered. Maybe I am on the wrong street and not in the right triangle. Just as I enter through the doorway, "Tainted Love" starts to play inside the stripper room. Maybe it isn't a stripper room, but that's what I am calling it. What the hell is with this song?

The hallway seems to be noticeably narrower and darker. Much darker. This is nothing at all like the passage I remember. The walls are jet black with only one little light in the center that barely lit the way. After walking about a hundred feet down into this dark square tunnel, there is finally a door.

Moans and screams fill the air from the other side. As I slowly open the door, I hear a couple fucking against the wall just outside the entry, and I look over to see a vampire towering over the hot blonde he has just slammed into the wall, with his fangs dug into her neck. Blood glistens in the reflection from the small light above as it trickles down the side to her perky, taut breast. Guess that explains where the sounds were coming from. Everyone walking about and acting as if nothing is happening, is the norm here.

Sex in the streets and vampires feeding on their slaves is just as common as sex in the bedroom for humankind. Our streets are more so pathways with chambers lining the way. Vampires can move at rapid speeds, so there is no need for vehicles here, other than the carts or motorcycles used to drive humans from place to place. The human body cannot withstand the warp speeds. Homes are built within the chambers and stacked depending on the depth of the ground above. Imagine it as a city on a smaller scale built beneath another town. Originally, the city built the chambers and passages as a way to secretly transport things during the war. It had been abandoned and believed to have been filled in and closed off to the outside world.

When my father and his coven were forced to leave their original homes, they came here looking for shelter. With no other place to go, they were forced to start their lives here beneath the city above. The tunnels we call passages go for miles and miles. Some even have been said to lead to New Orleans. I'm not sure this is true, since there's a distance of three hundred miles between the two cities. No sooner than the door closes behind me, my phone starts ringing. I don't recognize this number. It could be Austin, but I really can't talk to him before I talk to my parents and find out more information.

"You are running out of time," Austin's dad's voice yells loudly.

I have to shake off their voices, at least for now, until I find my dad. I have to figure out what is going on. Why does Austin need to be protected? What does he need protection from?

Chapter 5
AUSTIN

Thank God, I'm finally able to leave work. I run to the time clock machine that looks like it's from the 1970's to punch my card. I'm trying to get out of here before anyone sees me and asks me to do something else. Reaching in my pocket, I pull out the wadded-up piece of paper that has the chick's number on it.

"*Damn it*!" I swear under my breath when realize I don't even know her name. I got so thrown off by the "protect him, your parents sent me" bullshit, and maybe those damn blue eyes. I forgot to even to ask her what her name was. I hardly even said anything to her before I ran off into hiding.

Actually, I was a complete ass to her. Why would she not put her name on the paper with her number? Who just leaves someone a number without a name—although she might have told Stacy. I walk around the outside of the store, so the manager or Mr. Jones doesn't see me. Because even though I am clocked out, he will still ask me to do something.

There is a black SUV sitting in the back parking lot with two guys inside. They look like they just rolled in from some sort of space movie, dressed in all black and wearing sunglasses. I couldn't see their eyes, but I would swear that they're watching me. Nope, this isn't weird at all. The vehicle starts moving slowly as I walk closer to the front of the store. I speed up my steps to an almost running pace before I finally reach the door to go inside. Out of breath, I see Stacy standing there and tell her what just happened. The look on her face is not a look I was expecting from her.

"Austin! They're after you for a reason. I can't explain it to you, but you need to call Haley, and we need to find her as soon as possible. We have to get you out of here."

"What the hell is going on, Stacy?" I yelled at her.

I'm getting a little freaked out about all this. Why does this chick need to protect me, and why do I need to get out of here so quick?

"Austin, just breathe slow, deep breaths and listen to me. I was sent to work at the store to keep an eye on you. I am an Other!

She's making no sense at all to me. *Nothing* is making sense at this point. Still trying to catch my breath, I grab her by the arm, my next question coming out dumb, even to my ears.

"Just what the fuck is another?"

"No, Austin, I am an Other. As in a vampire. A daywalker." Stacy smirked

"Holy shit, are you crazy? There is no such thing as a damn vampire!"

"Austin, you have to listen to me! Calm down and Haley will explain everything later, but for now, we have to get you out of here quickly! I will distract them while you sneak out the back. Here are my keys, get in the back of my SUV and stay down. I will be out as soon as I get rid of them and clock out. Here's my phone, call Haley and tell her what's going on."

I may be freaking out a little, but I try to play it cool as I snatch the keys and phone from her hand and head for the back of the store. They still hadn't come in the front door yet, so I'm hoping they didn't see me come back into the store. Still wanting to be safe, I head out the back and slip into Stacy's backseat. This isn't weird at all, nope, not in the least. Okay, I need to try to focus so I can call this Haley chick. Damn, these girls are crazy as fuck—voices, vampires, men in black.

I pull Stacy's phone from my jacket pocket, along with the phone number on the crinkled piece of paper the name is written on. My hands are shaking as I push the digits, then I hear—"Sorry this person has a voice mailbox that has not been set up yet."

Why…just why the hell do people not have voice mail on their damn phones anymore! Finally, after what seemed like hours, I see Stacy coming toward the window on the driver's side. Then, I hear the popping sound from the key fob unlocking the doors. I think it has really only been less than ten minutes, tops, but that still seems like forever when you're just lying in the seat of a car, trying not to be seen. Thankfully, it's warmed up enough that I'm not freezing my ass off out here.

As soon as she pops her head into the car, I hear—

"Did you call Haley? She has to tell you what's going on Austin, I'm not allowed to. However, I can tell you that you are in danger and you have to believe everything we are telling you."

"Yes, I called her. She didn't answer, and there's no voice-mail set up on her phone. You guys are really freaking me the hell out. Stacy, I need to know what's going on."

Stacy starts the SUV and practically peels out of the parking lot.

"Austin, I'm not even sure what is going on, myself. I do know that those guys are the Thompson brothers and they're the ones who go after the hunters. I was only sent to work at the market to keep an eye on you. I was never really told why. Just that I had to keep watch and until today I didn't know that I was watching you for at all. Actually, I still have no idea really," Stacy says as she whips the car into a parking garage.

"Are you a hunter, Austin? Why would the hunters of the hunters hunt a non- hunter? Damn, that sounded confusing as hell!"

She then backed her car in between two other SUVs, as if we are trying to blend in.

"I have no idea what to even say at this point, Stacy! Haley has voices in her head, and you're talking about hunters. What the heck is a hunter? Do they go out and hunt people to feed you vampire folks? Need I even mention that fact? Is Haley also a vampire?"

"It's not my place to tell you what she is or isn't, Austin. You really do need to get in touch with her, but I'm sure she is most likely in the tunnels if she has no service on her phone. It's also possible she just has her phone off. Who knows? Oh, and no that is not what the hunters do!"

"Now you speak of tunnels, Stacy! Oh, and why the hell are we still sitting in this parking garage? We have been sitting here for almost an hour. Shouldn't we have moved on by now?"

"Shush, Austin! We have to wait, out of sight, until we can get ahold of Haley."

Well, Haley needs to answer her damn phone.

HALEY

I feel like I have been walking for miles down dark and dingy alleyways. Sex-crazed maniacs are on every corner, and noises poured from the darkness where vampires were feeding. Finally, I can see what looks like my parents' lair just a few feet ahead.

I can't believe I found it coming from the direction I did. I guess my instincts must have kicked in because I honestly had no idea where I was going or how I even got here.

I walk up to the door, which looks like a huge concrete stone covered in black paint, the color and texture of tar. A small window covered in bars centers it. I suppose the window is small to keep others out. I have no clue as to the purpose of the bars. Maybe it's just for looks. Thank God, I don't have to live down here. Reaching my arm up, I fit my hand between the bars and knock as hard as I can on the window. I know hitting on the concrete will accomplish nothing except break my knuckles, because it's soundproof.

After beating on the window for five minutes, my dad finally answers the door all six-foot-five inches of him. His long, stringy black hair is always flipped perfectly to the right side of his head. He has broad shoulders, and the darkest set of brown eyes. He still looks as young as he did the day he was turned, seventy-five years ago. Mother pops up behind him, so tiny in comparison. She is barely five feet tall, with short red hair and haunting blue eyes. I was born a year before my father turned her and claimed her as his mate. My fifteen-year-old brother Jonah pops out for a brief moment to say 'hi,' before he ran back to his room.

"Haley, why are you beating the door down? Is someone after you? Have you lost your mind? Are you okay? I thought we told you never to come down here alone," Dad fired off his questions in rapid, worried succession.

"Yes, Dad, I am okay. Losing my mind is an understatement, but I'm not technically alone. I have these damn voices that keep haunting me and will not shut the hell up. They say you know who they are and why I have to protect their son. I found the guy, but I think I may have really freaked him out when I showed up at his job and told him I was talking to his parents. Now that I think back on it, I would have been pretty freaked out, as well. I just really didn't know what to do, so that was my first thought. Guess it wasn't the best idea I've ever had."

I paused to take a breath.

"So here I am, hoping you and Mom might have some answers. These voices tell me their names are Dillion and Tonya Johnson, and I have to protect their son Austin. That's all they keep saying, over and over. They also tell me that I don't have much time."

"Haley these people you speak of are, well, they were hunters. They hunted and killed evil, rogue vampires and shifters. They maybe even murdered a witch or two. I have heard they got run off the road by those Thompson boys. The investigators wrote it up as driving while intoxicated and said Dillion lost control, running the vehicle off the road. I'm pretty sure the story rings true with these brothers running them off the road."

"They were never a threat to those of us who stayed

lowkey and brought our humans back here to feed. They always hunted down those who stalked humans like prey and feasted upon them until they were lifeless, or the ones who broke the code. Now, I don't know much about their son, Austin, as they always tried to keep him protected. As far as I know, he never knew what they did when they went out at night. I can tell you that Austin comes from a long line of hunters on his father's side. If I had to bet, those damn Thompson boys will be after him soon. Austin has no idea how much trouble he's in and the shit storm that's headed for him."

"Damn, Angelus, slow down and take a breath," Mom huffs. "How the hell can she take all this in with you talking so fast? Come in, Haley, and close the dang door."

"Oh, Celina, why do you always think no one understands me?" Dad replies.

"Mom, I totally understood every word he said. What I am not understanding, is why am I the one who has to help this guy?"

"Of course you understood him Haley, you were babbling just like him before he cut you off and started talking without catching his breath," Mom jokes.

"Haley, Celina, this is no laughing matter! This kid could be dead already, for all we know. He needs to be very careful and keep an eye out for trouble at all times. The brothers will not give up until they have what they want. Find him and try to convince him to come here. We will need to take this to Drake and the other Elders."

Drake is the eldest vampire in our coven. His sister, Eva, is next in line and then their brother Jareth.

"They will let us know what you need to do to protect and help Austin. I wish I had more answers for you, but I have never had to deal with anything like this. Sure, I have fought many fights, but not with the hunters of the hunters," Dad says in a stern voice.

"Okay, I'll head back to the store and hope he's still there."

"Please be careful, dear, and keep your eyes on everything around you at all times," Mom says, worry in her voice.

I left then, walking again for what seems like more miles than before, and then I finally reach the street. I look at my phone and notice three missed calls. Why is Stacy calling me so many times? I guess I should call her back. Damn! What is up with this song? Her ringtone is "Tainted Love."

"Hello!!" A guy's voice answers impatiently.

"Um, hello. I was trying to call Stacy, who is this?"

"It's Austin, who is this? Oh, never mind I see your name on the caller ID. Haley, we have been trying to get in touch with you for hours. Two guys showed up at my job looking like they just rolled out of a special agent movie. Stacy says they're some kind of killers who hunt the hunters. Well, I'm not a hunter and have no idea why *I* am being hunted. And how can you talk to my parents? Did you know Stacy is a vampire? Are you a vampire, Haley? What the hell is going on?"

"Austin, it's too much to explain over the phone. I will need you to come to me, and I'll explain everything then. Where are you?"

"I'm with Stacy, and we're hiding out in a parking garage on Travis Street."

While Austin proceeds to tell me where they are, it just dawned on me that I left my car back at the market.

"Austin, I'm sending you my location. I'm close by, over on Market Street. You guys come pick me up and take me back to Jones's Market to pick up my car. After that, you and I have to go on a trip to meet my parents," I explained.

"Meet your parents! Why do I have to meet your parents? We aren't dating, Haley!" Austin says, sounding more freaked out.

"Austin, I can't explain right now. You have to trust me, and I will fill you in on everything once I'm in the car with you."

"That's the same thing Stacy keeps saying over and over! I have to trust the two of you and should really listen to what you have to say. I'm willing to do so, but you must know how crazy and weird all this is to me. I'm just a homeless kid trying to find my way in life. Now, you all spring this shit on me with vampires, hunters, and tunnels—" Austin continued to rattle.

"You have to just stay calm, and everything will work out. Right now, I need you to give Stacy my location. I'm kind of just standing here, talking, when you guys could have already been here by now."

Austin begins to speak again as I hang up the phone and push it back into my pocket. I know it was a smartass thing to do, but I need to tell him everything in person because so much can be lost in translation on the phone.

Turning to face the street, I bumped into some guy walking past. "Excuse you! You should really watch where you're going," he says.

Once he touches me, I can hear the voice of someone around him. "Tell him to stop!"

"*Stop*!" I yelled at the stranger in the seconds before he almost steps out in front of a car speeding down Market street, straight through the traffic light which was red.

"Guess you should be watching where you are going, sir," I say with a slight smirk on my face.

The car comes to a screeching halt and then turns around to come back toward us. Damn it! It was Stacy. Why the hell is she speeding and not paying attention to the light? She pulls into the parking space right in front of where I'm standing and rolls the window down. I look around trying to find the stranger, but it's like he just disappeared. I don't see him anywhere.

"Oh my God, did I really almost hit that guy? I was just more focused on looking for you and totally didn't see the stop light," Stacy blurts out.

"Yes, you did Stacy. Thankfully, he had spirits with him yelling for me to stop him," I tell her as I climb into the back seat of her car.

"Thank God you were there. I don't know what I would have done if I would have hit him," Stacy replies, looking terrified.

"Just promise you're going to pay more attention with me in the car."

"Hurry Haley!" the voice of Austin's dad chimes in.

Chapter 7

AUSTIN

Wow. I had forgotten how beautiful this girl was until I turned around to look in the back seat. Looking her dead in the eyes, again, she makes the hair on my arms stand with a tingle. Those amazing cold blue eyes and that beautiful blonde hair, and she doesn't have the hoodie on hiding her perfect facial features anymore. Okay damn it, I'm staring at her, but it is again as if she has me in a trance. *Stop staring Austin! Just speak slowly.* I can hardly control myself—I'm feeling a little excitement in other places that I know are not appropriate at the moment. Okay, time to get it under control.

"So, um Haley, right?" I say with a slight smirk, or maybe it's a cheesy ass grin.

"Yes, it's Haley. You really should know that by now. "

Oh, now she has jokes.

"So, tell me, Haley, why am I being chased down by the rabid vampires? Speaking of which, I don't think it's a good idea to go back to the market for your car right now. I'm sure they are still around there looking for me. Maybe we can get Stacy to take us where we need to go, and we can come back for your car later."

"I don't think they will still be around there. I'm sure they think you ran by now and are scoping the city. We need to get my car, Austin, and find a way back into the tunnels without being seen. Stacy, do you mind taking us back to the market?" Haley asks.

Stacy, of course, agrees to drop us off, being the nice person that she is.

As we are pulling around to the parking lot, I see that the back-passenger side window has been broken out of my car. Great this is all I need. I have to sleep in this damn car, and I already can't run the heat for worrying about carbon monoxide poisoning. Now I have a busted window! Damn, I sound grumpy.

All the papers from my glovebox are scattered on the floorboard, not that I had much in there anyway. It's just that my mom's rings were in there, and they aren't there anymore. My clothes are all over the parking lot.

"I know we don't need to spend a lot of time here, Haley, but I have to get my car secured somehow. It's everything I own, which isn't a damn thing really, but what's valuable to me is inside this car."

I pick all of the papers up and notice that my birth certificate is also missing from the stack.

"Oh my God Austin, I am almost betting that the brothers took your birth certificate. Why they would need it, I'm not sure. They know the rings are of value to you. They most likely took them, knowing you would come after them. I hope you have your identification and Social Security card on you," Stacy chimes in.

Haley grabs me by the right arm and spins me so I am facing her.

"We have to hurry because we don't have much time. I know you want to secure your car, and you're worried about a lot of things right now. But Austin, we have very little time to waste and your parents' voices are getting fainter every time they speak to me. Your dad has been telling me over and over for the last two hours that we're running out of time."

"I can hardly hear your mom's voice at all anymore. 'Protect him' is all I get from her. When we get back to the tunnels and they know you are safe I could lose them forever. Sometimes, once they know their business is finished in this life, they will move on to the next peacefully, knowing that they didn't leave any unfinished business. I cannot imagine how crazy hard all this is for you to understand or even grasp all in one day. Stacy, do you know of any place that we can park his car out of the weather for a few days?" Haley finishes.

I finish picking up my things and put them into the trunk of the car with what other little belongings I have left.

"I have a friend who has a garage that his folks owned. He's been using it for his shop since he moved back here from New Orleans. I can call him and see if we can leave it there," Stacy replies.

Stacy makes the call, and her friend Rob says it's okay to leave my car there for a few days, or until I can return to pick it up. I take it he's also a daywalker from what I could hear of the conversation Stacy had with him on the phone. She filled him in on what was happening and the reason for me leaving my car.

We all get into our cars and drive a few blocks before pulling into Rob's place on the corner of Abel Street. The building looks like a service station from the 1950's that has been forgotten all too soon. The roll-up door is rusted and a fringe of what looks like the rope that is used to pull it down to close, hangs from the left side of the opening. The gas pumps are still here but are no longer in use. I don't think anyone has used them since the nineties from the looks of it. The whole place is covered in rust and peeling white paint. There's a sign barely hanging onto the building that says Jackson's Auto Service.

As soon as we get out of the car, we are met by this guy who is at least six feet two. He is dressed in coveralls with a long scraggly beard, and crazy looking brown hair all over the place, as if on purpose. His eyes are so dark you can hardly see his pupils, and his arms are huge.

He takes the towel out of his back pocket to wipe the grease from his hands before he reaches out to shake mine. He clutches my hand in a vice-grip. I try to grasp his back with the same force, but I know I have nowhere near the strength of this man.

"Hi, the name is Rob, Rob Jackson," he says with a husky, smoky tone to his voice.

"Austin. Nice to meet you Rob, and thank you for letting me leave my car here for a few days until we get all this crazy mess figured out."

"No problem at all, anything for a friend of Stacy's. It's nice to meet you too. I see you have a window broken out. That definitely looks like something those smart-ass Thompson boys would do. They are cowards, and they never fight alone. Two of the three are always together. The third one is too busy being a bloodsucker of the streetwalkers. The thing is, when you see them all together, shit is about to go down. I will look into the price of replacing this window for you. Now, I suspect you and Haley need to get going before those cats catch up with you," Rob says with a creepy ass look in his eyes.

"Yes, I suspect you're right, we do need to get moving. We

have to find an entry point to get back into the tunnels and to my parents' lair," Haley says to Rob.

"Now it's really getting ridiculous, did you just say your parents' *lair*?"

"Yes, Austin. That's what they call their home, but much unlike the lairs in stories you have read or heard of. This is like a normal home, like you and I live in. The tunnels under the city are filled with the lairs—I mean homes—of many vampires. I can assure you that you are in more danger walking the streets above the city than you will be in the tunnels," she says.

"So, you don't live in the lair with the vampires?" I ask her.

"No, I live in an apartment in Greenwood. Now get in and let's go!"

Getting into the passenger side of her car, I lean in and my arm brushes hers. It was like static electricity when we touched. Her eyes seemed as if they were getting even bluer, if that's even possible. She closes her door and turns the radio up with the song "Tainted Love" blasting in the speakers. It wasn't the older version from the 1960's, but the Marilyn Manson one which is so much better.

"I swear every damn where I go this song is playing, and it's driving me crazy, it's like the song is following me," Haley says.

"Haley, so you hear my parent voices. This is their song. They always said their love was tainted and sung it to each other all of the time. It's them who are playing the song every time you are around music. I have no idea why, unless they want to prove to me that it's them you are talking to. But I never knew why they always said their love was tainted. They just laughed it off, as if it were a joke. I supposed I should have questioned that more growing up."

"Austin, listen carefully, and please do not interrupt before I am finished," Haley says, as she looks at me with those damn eyes while pulling away from the garage onto the street.

Chapter 8
HALEY

S tarting the car, I wonder how I'm going to solve any of this. Why do I get this tingling feeling when I am around this guy? Just brushing his arm, a slight bit feels as if I have been shocked. I could feel a fire building behind my eyes. When I looked in the mirror, I had never seen my eyes that color blue before. Well, they were always blue, but this was electric blue. Playing it off, I turn the knob for the radio to play. That damn song "Tainted Love" again! Austin then explains to me that it was his parents' song and that's why I hear it everywhere I go. I guess that would explain this piece of the puzzle. Pulling onto the street, I decided to just let it out, no holds barred, balls to the wall, and tell him.

"Austin, listen carefully. I know it's far out there, and crazy shit is happening. You are only just beginning to see and hear crazy. Okay, so here goes. Your parents were night hunters, and very well-known ones. They always got the vampire, were, or whatever else they were hunting at the time. However, from what my dad says, they only chased rogue vampires and others who did not live by the code."

"A code? There is a code?" he questions.

"Yes. Now let me finish. Your parents did not just run their car off the road while drinking on a rainy night. My dad said he has heard stories in the Other World that they were pushed off the road by a rogue vampire. The Thompson brothers."

Austin, of course, flies off the handle after I say that.

"*I will kill them Haley. You hear me. I will f'ing kill them.*" He screams.

"Please, Austin! Calm down! You cannot kill them on your own. They're vampires and you're only human. You can't just go throw garlic on them, stab them in the heart with a stake, shoot them with a silver bullet and think they will die. That's not how this works. That's not how any of this works."

Wait! Did I just quote a damn TV commercial?

I'm losing my mind from all the voices in this damn city. If everyone could hear all the stuff that I listen to, they would have already gone crazy by the time they made it to my age. Austin manages to work out a laugh. Damn! That beautiful jawline stands out even more when he smiles.

"That's all my parents told me before they said I had to bring you back to go to the elders, hoping to figure out how to get you off the rogue vampire's most wanted list. It must be tough for you to have all this fall on you in one day."

"Haley, you have no idea. This morning, I was going about my normal worthless life. Now, I'm being chased by vampires, riding in the car with a vampire."

"Now, wait! I'm not fully vampire," I tell him. "I'm a dhampir, born of vampire and human. My brother, on the other hand, was born after Dad turned Mom. We will know if he becomes a vampire or will remain dhampir when he turns sixteen on the night of the harvest moon."

"Wow, this is all so confusing. I have no idea who is a werewolf, vampire, dhampir, or even human anymore. So, do you drink blood like the full vampires do, Haley?"

"No, I eat pretty much anything I want. I'm not a fan of fried foods at all. The smell of grease makes me sick to my stomach.

The stereotype is, however, correct about garlic, vampires nor dhampirs like it. While it doesn't necessarily kill either of us, it can make us severely ill, and some have been known to die. The only way to stop it, is to drink from the blood of the pure. Though, it's getting harder to find that in this day and time without drinking the blood of a child. In the vampire world this is normal with so many dhampir children growing up knowing who they are, and then they do not drink from the child. The finger is pricked, then the blood is harvested and kept by the Elders. The Elders are keepers of many things."

"I don't know much of what the Elders do. I came to live in the world with you humans once I was eighteen, and my parents said it was to protect me. So much for being protected, huh? Now, I'm being chased by these asshole brothers right alongside your homeless ass."

"Damn, Haley! Just blatantly call me 'homeless' why don't you?" he says.

"Sorry, that is not how I meant it, Austin. Why are you homeless anyway, if you do not mind me asking?"

"Now that you ask, I don't even know the real answer, Haley. My dad claimed he only had my grandmother and great-grandmother on his side who have both since died. My mom's family are all a bunch of assholes who want nothing to do with me because I am mixed. But now, I'm starting to think these were all lies as well. I've never seen any of my family members on either side. Do I even have other family members at all?"

"My parents and I moved here right before they had the accident and we always moved from one town to the next, so that was nothing new to me. I had made plans to go to State, but they left me with nothing other than the life insurance they had. The money barely covered their funeral costs. I did see some people at the funeral home who claimed to be my mom's family, but they never spoke to me and left before she was even buried."

"So, Haley, I have no idea at this point what's real anymore. Why am I homeless? Well, because I have no family to turn to. Working two days a week at the market doesn't pay much rent," Austin finishes speaking and just looks at me with a blank stare.

I can't turn to look at him because I'm driving and don't want to take my eyes off the road. I reach over and put my hand on his shoulder, trying to offer some comfort, but damn it almost hurts to touch him. I can feel heat, where my hand is touching his shoulder and again it's like static flows down my arm. I play it off and start to speak.

"I'm sorry Austin, I had no idea you were going through all of that when I started looking for you. You parents could only tell me where you were and what you looked like. After that, all I can get from them is, 'You have to help him.' So, here I am, helping you."

"Do you feel that, Haley? When you touch me, it's as if I'm being shocked by static electricity, but in a good way," Austin says, like he didn't give a shit about me being here to help him.

"I feel it, sort of," I reply, still trying to play it off as I move my hand. "Did you not care that I said I was here to help you? How about this? I know you have had a lot going on today, and it's getting late. Let's go back to my place where we can shower, get some rest, and have a fresh start tomorrow. You can sleep on my sofa. That has to be a lot better than the back seat of your car."

Did I really just invite this guy back to my house? What the hell is wrong with me?

"Thank you, but I don't want a pity party."

"I can assure you, there's no pity coming from me. I just know how long it takes to get through the tunnels to my family's place, and it's much farther to the Elders. I can find the passages with no problems, but I think we'll be better starting fresh tomorrow. I'm sure the Thompson brothers are out hunting for the night. They may be daywalkers, but from what I hear, they like to prowl at night and get up to no good. I'm sure that's why they were after you today," Haley reasoned.

"Okay, you're driving anyway, so I have to go where you take me. I could just jump out of the moving vehicle, but I don't see that happening," he laughs.

"But, please promise no more saying sorry, Austin."

I can't help but let out a little giggle because he was trying to be so serious while joking about jumping out of the car at the same time.

"You've got it, ma'am, no more pity party or *I am sorry* coming from me. So, we both agree to go back and get some rest for the night?"

"I'm good with that, sleeping on a sofa will be better than my car or the shelter cot for sure, as long as I am not putting you out," Austin replied.

"You aren't putting me out at all. As long as you know, it's just so you can rest and clear your head for the night, nothing more. Shake on it," I say, reaching my hand out to him.

Holy shit! This time it's even stronger! I can feel the heat when he took my hand to shake it. I pull away quickly and have to admit to him what I thought at that time.

"Damn Austin, what are you doing when you touch me? Why does it feel like we are shocking each other?" I ask him.

"I was hoping you were feeling that also. From the first time—when you walked into the store, you were barely close to me, but I could feel the hair on my arms standing on end. I thought it was maybe just my nerves, but earlier your eyes changed color when my arm brushed you. When you put your hand on my shoulder, it was stronger. Just now, when you shook my hand, it felt like it was burning. I don't think it's me, I'm not the one with any powers here, Haley," he says.

"Maybe I should just stop touching you until we meet with the Elders tomorrow to find out what's going on. I wouldn't want anyone going into combustion because I touched them. We should find food before we get to the apartment, mostly because I want to touch the person's hand at the drive-thru window to make sure it isn't just me."

He agrees.

We exit off Highway 20 and pull into an Arby's a few blocks from my apartment. Pulling up to the speaker, I order our food and drive around to the window. When the cashier takes my cash, I make sure to place it in his hand, so my finger touches him. I felt no static. Nothing. I'm thinking there has to be more to Austin's story and that there's part of his life that was kept from him. He has some kind of power. There's no way I would have these feelings otherwise. I get lost in thought while we're waiting for the food.

"Hey! Why are you so quiet now, where did you just daze off to? More voices talking to you, Haley?"

"No, I was just thinking," I reply, while reaching for the bag of food.

"Here, grab this." I shove the bag into his lap, making sure not to touch him this time.

"Okay, damn. I will leave you be the next time you have a spaced-out moment. You don't have to slam the food into me," he laughs.

"Oh, you shithead! I didn't mean to shove it so hard, guess I did get kind of lost in my thoughts. I'll pay more attention next time."

"Are we close to your apartment by any chance because I really have to pee," Austin says.

"Yes, we are only a couple of blocks away. My place is up one-third level, so try not to pee yourself before we get up the stairs."

I've only been around him for a few hours, yet I feel very comfortable with him. It feels like I've known him for years.

"Haley, hurry," the voices say again.

"Austin, your parents are telling me to hurry again, but I still don't think it's a good idea to go tonight."

"Neither do I," he says.

Chapter 9

AUSTIN

Haley puts her hand on my shoulder to comfort me after I tell her why I'm homeless and have no clue about my fucked-up family. Once she touched me, I felt as if I had been struck by lightning. It was as if a fire was being lit inside me and all the rage I had built up floated away. I could feel it burning from her touch. I knew she felt it too, but she took her hand away as if nothing happened.

Is it because she's a dhampir and that happens when she touches a human? So many questions running through my head.

"Austin?" She shakes me from my thoughts. "Let's go back to my place where we can shower, get some rest, and get a fresh start tomorrow. You can sleep on my sofa, that has to be a lot better than the back seat of your car."

Holy shit. Did she just ask me to stay with her for the night—oh wait, she said on the sofa, damn it! I feel myself getting hard in my joggers, and I have to put my hands in my lap to cover it.

Haley reaches her hand out for the promise to stay on the sofa handshake, and the moment our hands touch, it's even stronger this time—the fire, the burn, the shock! She snatches her hand away as if I had squeezed too hard, but it had to be the shockwave of energy that was running through us that caused her to move away so quickly. This day is getting more bizarre by the hour.

After stopping for food, we finally make it back to her apartment. I have to run up the stairs, hoping she's running behind me to unlock the door before I pee myself.

"Damn Austin, are we running a sprint?" Haley asks, topping the stairs.

"I told you I had to pee," I reply, laughing at her while she opens the door, and I run past her. Then it hits me that I have no idea where her bathroom is.

"Down the hall, first door on the left," she says. She must have known by the look on my face that I had no idea. Thank the lord and all that is holy, I finally get to the bathroom and do my thing. Coming out, I see Haley standing at the bar between the small kitchen and living room, eating her food. I can't say it enough just how beautiful she is, and the way her eyeliner frames her eyes...

It's a damn trap, that's what it is—once you look into them, you're locked there until you shake yourself away, which is what I have to do.

"I put your sandwich and fries on a plate for you, and there's ketchup in the fridge if you want it," she says, nodding to my food.

I grab my plate and squirt ketchup all over my fries, then turn back around to face her on the other side of the bar.

"So, what's the plan for tomorrow, Haley? Um, wait. I don't even know your last name."

"My last name is silly, Austin, and I don't want you making fun of me so you don't need to know it," she replies with that cute ass grin on her face.

"It can't be any worse than mine, Johnson! I mean, that's what guys call their cocks, Haley. Now, how can your last name be worse than that?"

"Okay fine, it's Devile," she says.

My jaw may have dropped open with my hand putting a fry halfway into my mouth. "Your name is devil, like the dark angel turned from the heavens and into the leader of hell, devil?"

"Well, that's what most people think, but it's pronounced Deville. We may be part of the dark side, but we for sure don't have part of the devil's doings—well, other than the sinful ways, but not devil's, no. Now that you have that to joke about, my dad's name is also Angelus, so there—his name is Angel Devil," Haley says, trying to play it off as a joke.

"*Wow*! I actually think that's pretty awesome. How many people would love to have a badass name like that?"

"Ha, right. I should have known you would like it! Most guys think it's a badass name. I didn't get a cool name, just a basic American girl name—Haley—how uncool is that name?" She shrugs.

"But you still have a badass last name. Okay, let's get off the names for a bit, what's your game plan for tomorrow?" I ask.

"We have to go back into Shreveport pretty early in the morning, and find a passageway that's closest to my parent's lair. Once we're there, they will lead us to the Elders. When we get before the Elders, we'll have to tell them everything and try not to leave out any details you can remember about your childhood. They will decide if the Thompson brothers will be brought to trial, which I'm one hundred percent sure will happen—because once they know the brothers are after you, they'll know the rumors have to be true," she replies.

I move from the bar stool into the living room to sit on the dark brown leather sofa. Before I sit down, I place my drink onto the coaster next to a romance novel she has sitting on her wooden coffee table.

"So, this is where I will be sleeping tonight? It's for sure better than the back seat of a Nissan." I asked her, the whole time thinking how much better it would be if I was sleeping in her bed.

"Yes, sir, that would be the place. Are you ready to sleep already? If so, I'll grab you a pillow and a blanket from my room. I'm about to go shower and change into my night clothes. I can grab you one anyway since I will be in there already," Haley replies.

I then remember I didn't grab any clothes out of my car before we left the garage.

"I'll be up for a while; do you mind if I take a shower? I'll need to throw my clothes in the wash, and maybe cover myself with a blanket until they are done. I forgot to get clothes out of my car before we left it," I tell her, feeling like a complete dumbass.

"You can shower in the hall bath when I'm done with my shower. I may have some shorts you can wear. I sleep in men's gym shorts because they tend to fit looser," she says while heading back toward the front of the apartment, opening a door across from the kitchen that I must have missed on the way in. I'm guessing that's the master bedroom.

"I'll be out shortly," she grins as she walks through the door, closing it behind her.

I pull off my shoes and place them on the floor next to where I'm sitting before letting back the reclining part of the sofa. My mind starts to wonder about why these brothers were after my parents in the first place. There has to be more to this story than just, your parents were hunters so they had to die by the hands of rogue vampires. They were good people, but they did always seem to have a lot of secrets and kept me away from their room, leaving it under lock and key while they were out of the house. Which is weird because after they passed away, their room was totally bare other than their clothes and personal belongings. What could they have been hiding from me? Where did it go *if* they were hiding anything from me?

I must have drifted off to sleep, not even realizing that forty-five minutes had passed, when I heard a door slam, and noticed Haley standing in front of me with a black tank top and gym shorts, holding a pair of her other gym shorts in front of my face. Damn, this woman is fine, and she smells a-fucking-mazing.

Grinning and wiping my eyes, I reach for the shorts.

"Thank you, they look rather small for me, Haley," I tell her.

"I think they will fit just fine until your clothes are done in the wash. Here's a blanket, and the things you need for a shower are already in the bathroom closet. Throw me your clothes outside the door and I'll toss them into the washing machine," Haley replies.

I turn the water on before putting my clothes outside of the door, getting it just the right temp. I stand in the shower, letting the water run over me as my mind starts to wander again. This time it's not on my parents, or the things that have happened today. It's now on how good Haley looked in those shorts. I feel myself getting hard, closing my eyes and picturing her out of those shorts, and how good her tits looked in that damn shirt. I reach for my cock, squeezing it tight with my right hand, letting the hot water bounce against the head.

Man, I'm so damn horny, but I don't want to do this in her shower. I want it to be in her bed. It's been almost six months since I have had sex at all. I can't very well get myself off in a car either. Well I could, but you never know when someone will walk by or peep into the window.

Gripping myself harder, I feel myself stiffening even more, and I reach for some conditioner for lube. Yes, this is a thing guys do in the shower. I start moving my wrist up and down, making long, slow strokes. Massaging the head when I reach the tip, I open my eyes and look down at my throbbing hard cock, slick from the conditioner. Wishing Haley was on her knees in front of me, I pinch my nipple with my left-hand, taking turns from the left to the right. I'm not sure if this is a thing all guys do, but I've found it makes me even more horny.

As I start stroking faster and faster, flashes of her hot lips on my cock run through my mind. Her taking me deep into her throat. The smell of the conditioner lubing my cock reminds me of her sweet scent. I can feel her licking her way up my torso as I rub my hand up my body. Her lips clasping onto my nipple, as I pinch it again. At the thought of her kissing me while I slide myself deep inside her and fucking her right here in the shower, the strokes come faster. It isn't long before I feel my orgasm creeping up from my balls. I let out a loud moan, which I'm sure she could hear in the other room, releasing my load onto the shower floor. Feeling a little light headed now, I finish my shower quickly, dry myself off, and put on the shorts that I was given to wear.

They're a little tight on my still semi hard dick. I sure as hell hope we don't have to run out of here quick while I am wearing these, with no shirt on and these damn little shorts.

I finally finish up in the bathroom and return back to the

living room where Haley is now sitting on the sofa, wrapped in a blanket. I grab the other blanket she brought in for me and cover up fast enough I hope she didn't notice how tight the shorts were. I for sure have to control myself not to get hard while I'm sitting on the sofa with her—at least until I get my pants back on.

Chapter 10
HALEY

I have to play it cool around Austin tonight. I honestly have never been before the Elders. I've only seen them in passing and heard stories of them from my parents. I can't let him know that I have no idea what's going to happen. I do know there have to be more pieces to this puzzle and hopefully we can find some answers when we meet tomorrow.

I have seen the brothers, Bristol, Brandon, and Brock, and had no idea they were so evil until recently. We even played together as children growing up, until our teenage years and they moved away from the Other World.

They definitely became men once they hit their twenties. All of them were just as muscled and toned as the other, but oddly none of them look alike. Bristol has blond hair, green eyes, and a short stocky build. Brandon is brunette, with blue eyes and a tall muscular build. Brock has sandy blond hair with a hint of strawberry blond, and hazel eyes, with I guess you would say more of a swimmer's build. All three were sexy as hell.

"Shit!" Why am I thinking about them while I'm in the shower?

I rush to get out of the shower and shake the three brothers and their muscles from my thoughts. Why would I think of them when I have this hot ass guy sitting on my sofa?

I slide on a pair of shorts from my dresser and grab the biggest pair I have for Austin to wear while I wash his clothes. Throwing on the black tank top that was laying on my bed, I removed the towel from my head and shook my hair out. Before leaving the room, I look in my closet, getting Austin the pillow and blanket that I promised him.

Returning to the living room, I see it looks like Austin has become comfortable and dozed off. I walk over and wave the shorts over his face. Without me even saying a word, his eyes pop open and he acts as if he's wide awake.

Wiping the sleep from his eyes, he says, "Thank you, they look rather small for me, Haley."

I assure him they will be just fine and fit him okay until his clothes are done in the wash, telling him also where the things he needs for his shower are as he gets up and heads toward the bathroom. Once he goes in and closes the door, I don't want to feel weird just standing outside the door waiting for him to hand me his clothes, so I go to the kitchen like I'm getting something from the cabinets.

All the while, I'm glancing at the door, waiting for him to open it and place his clothes outside of it. When he did, he had the towel wrapped around him so I only got a peek, but those damn abs caught my eye right away. I waited for him to close the door completely before moving to get his clothes. I take them back to my bathroom where the washer and dryer are, locking the bedroom door behind me. I place his clothes in the wash, add detergent, and close the lid. I can smell him on his clothes, damn he smells so manly, and the thought of rubbing those abs comes to mind.

I have a few minutes while he's in the shower. So, I lay on the bed and take my little friend from the nightstand. I place it on the bed bedside me, rubbing my clit with my fingers. I'm already wet just thinking about Austin and those damn eyes staring back at me. Again, his abs come to mind. I want to lick every inch of them so bad, I can almost taste him on my tongue. The smell from his clothes still lingers in my senses.

I grab the silver bullet from the bed beside me and turn it on the low setting to start with, placing it on my clit where my fingers were seconds before. My thoughts wander to Austin being on top of me, taking me, pushing himself deeper and faster inside of me, as I increase the speed. The moment that thought hit me, and the feeling of his abs brushing against my torso, I can see his jawline clinching. I can hear him telling me I'm his. My climax is building, I feel the fire from his touch, I see sparks behind my eyes, and I finally release myself.

"Oh my God, Austin," I say out loud. I couldn't help it.

My body goes limp, but I know I have to get myself together before he's out of the shower. Pushing myself up from the bed, I slide my shorts back on and try to get my hair looking right again. Pulling it back in a ponytail is my best bet. *Do guys really notice these things, anyway*? I think to myself, looking into the closet for another blanket. The fuzzy white one was the first one I grab, wrapping it around me as I leave the room to go sit on the sofa.

Not long after, Austin comes out of the bathroom wearing my shorts, which are short shorts on him, his little ass peeking out the bottom just a bit before he covers it with the blanket but, that's not the first thing I notice. I get the full view of those abs now, and damn he's blessed. I think I gave him truth shorts, because they sure are telling everything he has. Why did he have to put the blanket over it? I was enjoying the view, and what a nice view it was. At least he doesn't have a shirt to cover his abs with.

"How was your shower?" I ask him, trying to pretend I'm not staring at him.

"It was much needed. I have been having to take showers at the shelter and at the truck stop. Having a real shower was nothing short of amazing. By the way, I told you these shorts were going to be too small. My ass is hanging out the back, and my manhood barely fits in the front," Austin jokes.

I can't even imagine not having my own shower, or a place to sleep for that matter. I don't say this out loud, of course—I would never say anything that he may take the wrong way. The little voice in the back of my head—not the one from the other side; one like we all have in the back of our heads—is telling me I should let him just stay here until we get this all figured out. Another is telling me this is not a good idea because I may not be able to keep my hands off of him, even if it hurts to touch him.

I laugh at him and say, "You look good in the shorts Austin, but I agree they may be a bit too small."

Oh my God, did I just tell him he looks good in the shorts? I'm losing my damn mind.

He just laughs it off and sits down on the other side of the couch, and I'm sure I'm blushing

Suddenly my phone rings, and I pick it up, seeing Stacy's name on the caller ID.

"Haley, it's Stacy. Rob called me and said the Thompsons just came by looking for Austin. They saw his car sitting outside earlier when they drove past. He told them he didn't know who the guy was who brought the car in, and threatened to shift into his wolf if they didn't leave. I just wanted

"Austin, I'm going to bed. I know you're worried, but try to get some sleep. We have more crazy shit to deal with tomorrow," I tell him

"I doubt I'll get much sleep, but I'll try. Goodnight, Haley," he says with that damn smirk again. I swear it gets me every time.

"If you need anything to drink or snacks, just make yourself at home. Goodnight Austin," I say before going into my room and falling asleep.

The dreams—they come so vivid. I see Austin's parents being chased by a truck. All three of the brothers are there. They go faster, faster, the truck rams them in the side, and then suddenly Austin's dad's face comes into clear view. His eyes are staring dead into mine, and that's when I wake up.

"Don't worry dear, the truth will come out tomorrow." The faint voice of Austin's mom rings in my ear.

Chapter 11

AUSTIN

After Stacy's call, I have become even more worried. I think the reality just set in. I'm only human, I have no extra strengths to take on these rogue vampire brothers. I tossed and turned all night, my mind racing, full of what ifs. I think I may have been asleep for around two hours when I hear Haley yell.

"Austin! We have to leave now!"

The yell of my name alone was enough to shake me from my sleep. "What the hell is going on? Why are you yelling, and why do we have to go now?"

"I spotted one of the brothers snooping around in the parking lot. If we put you in a hoodie, maybe they won't recognize you. I don't think they have a clue who I am," she replies.

I lift myself up from the sofa, wiping the sleep from my eyes, and take the hoodie Haley hands to me. I walk to the bathroom, trying to avoid her seeing my morning wood. I know I should be in a hurry, but I don't think it's going to matter how fast we leave if he's still in the parking lot. How the hell are we supposed to get out of here without being seen? Maybe this hoodie will disguise me enough. Maybe it's the brother that wasn't one of the two back at the market.

Once I'm done in the bathroom, I walk out to find Haley waiting on me at the door.

"Come on, he's in the parking lot behind the apartments. I think we can leave now and he won't see us," she tells me.

Rushing down the stairs, we make it to her car quickly. Just as I look over my shoulder, this huge guy comes running across the parking lot.

"Go, Haley. Get the hell out of here," I yell as soon as I slam the car door. Another guy comes around the other side of the car, tapping on her window.

She lets off the brake, yanks the Camaro into gear and floors it, leaving them running behind us. "Is it true what they say about vampires, Haley? Do they have Superhuman speed?" I ask her. I'm pretty sure I sound stupid, but hell. I have no clue.

"It's true for some, not all," she replies

Whatever that's supposed to mean. I just kind of nod my head and ask, "Do you think they can catch us on foot?"

She shrugs her shoulders and just shoots me a look. I know one thing is for certain, I'm scared of those fuckers following behind us. They were following in the SUV behind us as we make the turn to get onto the highway.

"Haley, they're right behind us, we have to lose them," I tell her.

She hands me her phone and tells me to call Stay. "Tell her we need Rob to call his pack. We need their speed and animal instincts."

"A pack? Like a gang? Wait, you said animal instincts. What the hell, Haley!"

She just looks at me and grins a little. "Just call, Austin. We need them to distract the brothers, so we can get away and into the passageway."

They pull up beside us, trying to push us over, but Haley is quick to respond, avoiding us getting hit. I look at the gages and she is over ninety miles per hour now. I searched the phone for Stacy's number, calling her and getting her voicemail every damn time.

"She is not answering." The moment I said it, Stacy called me back. I let her know what's going on and tell her we need Rob's pack to distract them, but not before I ask just what kind of pack we're talking about here.

Laughing, she says, "They're werewolves, Austin."

Well, shit just got a little stranger. We're calling on wolves to save us from vampires, driving ninety miles per hour down a highway. How could this week get any weirder?

Actually, I might not want to know the answer to that.

Stacy lets me know she'll inform Rob, and he should have the guys here in no time. "He loves fucking with those brothers," she tells me.

"Thank you, Stacy," I reply before hanging up.

A few miles before getting into Shreveport, I see a truck come between us and the bothers' SUV, then another truck beside it and yet another behind it. They have the SUV boxed in. I then see Stacy coming up beside us in the left-hand lane, waving her arm out the window.

I pick up the phone to call her again. "How the hell did you guys get here so fast?" I ask her.

"I was already on the highway coming into town. When I called Rob, he was just across the Texas state line with some of his pack. They were headed back to his shop to work on a hot rod they picked up. Now enough about all that. You and Haley have to hurry. I'll be at the shop with the guys, after they're done taking those assholes on a little detour. Tell Haley to take Highway Forty-Nine, and turn on King's Highway. There's a passage in the bookstore across from the college. I'm hanging up now so I can focus on the road and distracting these fuckers behind us."

I nod my head out the window toward her, and once again relay the information to Haley. She knows exactly where the bookstore is, and we turn on King's Highway with not a Thompson in sight. We pass the store, looking for somewhere to park, but we don't see anything open.

"We have to find some place to try to get the car off the street," Haley says. We turn onto Alexander Avenue, then right into an alley that goes behind the bookstore. There are cars parked in a small parking lot back here, and then Haley says, "There's the symbol on that door."

She pointed at a door just off to the side of the building. The door is painted black, but I don't see the symbol that she's pointing to. "Haley, there is no symbol on that door," I tell her.

"Oh, it's there. Only dhampir and vampires from the Shreveport coven are able to see them, other than the humans whom have been allowed to return to the city without an escort. Those humans are the mates or slaves of members of our coven."

We park the car, both putting the hoodies on over our heads before walking up to this random black door on a brick and mortar building. All of the other doors are painted battleship grey, but not this one—nope, it's jet black.

It's still rather cold out this morning, and the wind is making it even colder. Luckily, we don't have to walk too far. Haley reaches to knock on the door, but before she could get her hand on it, the door opened on its own. On the other side stood an old, frail lady, holding a notepad in her left hand and a pencil in the other.

"I knew you two were coming, they told me so," the lady says with a screech in her tone.

"Who are *they*?" I ask her.

"Oh, a friend of your father's young man, nothing to worry about. Come along now," she says before putting her pad down on the table beside the door before placing her left hand on my back and her right hand onto Haley's. "You kids need to get moving now, your way is just down those stairs." She picks up the stick that I thought was a pencil earlier, and taps it on the outside of the door, and it turns the same color as the others, battleship grey. My mouth drops open in awe of her making it magically change colors.

"Um, Haley, did you see that?" I ask her.

She then replies, "Of course I saw it. She's a witch. Her name is Mrs. Hyde, I've met her a few times when I came here to pick up books. She just disguised the door. No one will be able to follow us once she closes it back."

Walking down the stairs, the lights start to dim, and at the bottom of the stairs there's another door. Something falls on the floor behind us—it sounds like metal hitting concrete.

"Sorry, I forgot to give you the key for the door," Mrs. Hyde yells. I turn and see the key and bend to pick it up.

Haley says, "It won't work for you, I have to open it. Once we're inside, it will lock behind us. I'll keep the key until we return it later."

Once the door closes behind us, it's almost completely dark, with only a few small lights above us lighting the way. Haley takes my hand, guiding me along the way. "We're safe here Austin, at least for now anyway."

What the hell did she mean, *for now*?

Chapter 12

HALEY

Once we lose those asshole brothers and find the door into the passage, I can finally let out a sigh of relief. You have no idea how happy I was to see Mrs. Hyde on the other side of that door. She has always been so welcoming and she's a great friend to my family and me.

I lead Austin down the stairs and into the passageway. I can see he's not very comfortable, and I probably shouldn't have told him we were safe for now. Instead, I tried to make it sound like we were safer than we were before coming down here. Once we're deeper into the tunnels away from the bookstore, we'll be on our own.

For the most part, nothing bad happens down here other than a few humans getting lost because they were trying to find their way out after sneaking away from the vampire they fucked the night before. However, sometimes those humans never find their way back out. Female vampires will also kill the humans who sleep with the vampire they claim to be their man, and same with the males who sleep with their women.

It's the same for the men that sleep with the ladies' men, and vice versa. This is after all the otherworld, and all kinds of sex goes down here. Just from time to time we have those who stake their claim and don't want to share them with anyone else, resulting in the random human found drained in the passageways.

I honestly *do* think we're safe coming in this way. But whether we are or not, I can't show any fear in my facial expressions. The last thing I need is to freak him out before we even get to the Elders.

I grab Austin by the shirt, trying to avoid skin contact. We walked into the dark hallway, this one narrower than the one I had to go into yesterday. He looks like he's scared shit-less, but trying to be brave with me. The lights get dimmer as we go deeper down the into the passage.

"Austin, it will be better once we get into the tunnels. We're only in the small passage leading us down into the otherworld," I assure him.

After walking another hundred feet or so, I can see the opening up ahead. I just have to figure out which way to go once we get into the opening. I know that the lairs are on the other side of town on the street level, but the tunnels run right through the middle of the city, and down each side.

"I think if we take a right here, we'll just have to walk straight forward. It could be a few miles of walking. I hope you have your walking shoes on," I tell him, wishing I hadn't worn these boots this morning.

"Yeah this is going to suck for you in those boots," he replies with a laugh, saying just what I was thinking. Thank God they're my flatter boots, rather than my high heeled ones. Lord knows I'd be walking on my bare feet before we got to my parents' lair if that were the case.

The temperature seems to keep dropping the farther we get underground. It also seems to be getting darker, which is kind of odd. I don't remember it being this dark when I was here before. Maybe a light was out, or one of the openings from above could be blocked. Suddenly I hear voices, people talking. I can't tell if it's people of our world or if I'm hearing them from the other side.

It's a chant, and I can't make out the words clearly. The closer we get, the words *stop now* become clearer. Over and over they keep chanting it. *Stop now. Stop now. Stop now.* Then I hear it all clear as day. *Stop now. Stop now. Stop now. You are in danger. Turn back now!* But I have no idea where or from whom the voices are coming from, or what direction, for that matter.

I turn to Austin. "Do you hear those voices?"

"What are you talking about, I don't hear shit but the water dripping from above, and something that sounds like street noise," he replies.

So now I know it's someone from the other side, but who? It sounds like a child. This is really not something that I have heard before. It's normally a straight forward message from the person, letting me know what their purpose is. Never a chant. Never like they were crying.

"Dude, it sounds like they're crying, they're telling me to stop now, and that we're in danger," I tell him and grab him by the arm. *Wow*. This time, even with the fabric covering his skin, I can feel it. It's electric and I can't let go of him. My hand has his arm gripped tight, like a magnet attracted to metal.

I try to pull way, but it's forcing me to stay. I move my body closer to his and look him in the eyes. His green eyes have a slight glow to them now.

"Haley, you have a tight grip there, but I can feel your energy! It's like you have a current, a power of sorts, and it's running through my body from your hand," he tells me before I'm finally able to release my grip on his arm.

"What the hell was that?" I ask him.

"I have no idea, but you just had total control over me. I was frozen in place and your eyes hypnotized me," Austin replied.

Suddenly the chanting stopped, and I hear the voice loudly say, "*Enough*! I'm Austin's grandmother. You must listen, child. You two are in for dangerous paths ahead. You have no idea what you're getting yourself into, young lady. I tried to scare you back with the chanting. I'm no voice from the other side, and I'm very much alive. I'm telepathic, I knew contacting you would be better than Austin for the time being as he thinks I'm dead. Austin has no idea what lies in his family's past, or what he is destined to become. You two have much to learn and it shall happen quickly. I'll stay with you in spirit until you've reached your family. Then you must go to the Elders at once. You can't tell Austin you've heard from me until after you've met with the Elders and he's found out the truth. Now get moving."

"What the hell are you looking at over there? You've just been staring at the wall for at least five minutes. Did you know you do that a lot, Haley?" Austin asks, breaking me from the trance I was in as I listened to the voice claiming to be his grandmother.

"We need to get moving. The longer we stay still, the more time we give those assholes to catch up," I tell him without answering his question.

Chapter 13
AUSTIN

I swear we've been walking for miles when Haley suddenly grabs me by the arm and looks me in the eyes, looking like she's seen a ghost. I mean, she does talk to them after all, so who's to say she can't see them? Once she grabs my arm and our eyes lock, it's like I can feel her energy, a current running from her hand, throughout my body down to my feet, and back out into her hand. She releases her grip and just stands in front of me, staring at the wall for five minutes, still locked in whatever trance she put me in. All I can do is stare at her while she's staring at the wall.

When I'm finally able to speak, I ask her, "What the hell are you staring at?"

"We have to get moving. The longer we stay still, the more time we give those assholes to catch up," she tells me, grabbing my shirt and pulling me forward while she takes off speed walking.

"Haley, what's going on? Why are we suddenly in a hurry? Did you hear something? Why did you ask me if I heard it?"

She looks away. "I thought I heard something, but I think my mind is playing tricks on me. I just know we don't have much time before the brothers find out where we are. They have killer instincts and can hunt us down in a matter of minutes. And, I wasn't staring at the wall. I was thinking about where we had to go from here," she says while pulling my shirt even harder. I knew from the look on her face she was lying and there's something she isn't telling me. Something she saw or heard.

While she's pulling me forward, I take a moment to notice how beautiful she really is and her ass, *oh my God*! Her ass is amazing. It's all I can do to not pull her back and wrap her in my arms. I just want one moment with her. To hold her, to kiss her, to grab a handful of that ass.

I've only known her for a few days but it feels like forever. It feels like we're already a couple and have been dating for years. Which is weird to me—I've never felt this way about anyone I've dated. Even ones I dated for more than a few months. I feel like there's a bond. A force between us. When she grabbed me, it was as if I had no more control over my body, my movements. I was her puppet. Like some sort of spell had been put on me and there was no way I could break loose from it.

"We need to take a right here, I think, and it should only be another mile or so before we reach the city lairs," Haley said, once again knocking me from my thoughts.

"Tell me more about this city of lairs you speak of. You said before it was like houses us humans live in, only they're dens underground?" I inquire.

"Yes, it's just like a street in town, only much narrower. The dens line each side of the tunnels going one way, and shops going the other. Shops down here are very different from the ones above us on the streets, however. They run towards vampire needs," she snorts with a giggle.

"Vampire needs, huh? I mean, what more does a vampire need other than blood, and a place to sleep during the day?"

I probably shouldn't have asked that question—not after hearing the answer she gave.

"Well, they need condoms, because vampires can still get humans pregnant. Nonmetal chains for the dominate ones, sex toys, that kind of stuff, and that's just the sex shops. Then there are the feeding bars where live humans come to let them feed. For those looking for something more exotic, they have a blood list, of many animals, and famous humans who make money from selling their blood. It's somewhat like the beer list in our bars in the city. We won't discuss the raw meat selections they have available." She gags a little before she continues.

"There's a strip club, and a grocery store where meat and blood can also be bought for in home use. Not all vampires like to feed in pubic, or in the open at all for that matter. You'd be surprised how many of them purchase blood to keep from feeding on the living. Well, I suppose they're still living, but they donate the blood. The animal blood comes from the slaughter houses after processing the meat for supermarkets. We have many people in the outside world who supply the Other World, Austin. I could go on about the shops and such, but you'll see it all when we arrive. It is a two or three-mile strip in the tunnels. The Elder's chambers sit at the end of the strip. It's the only place the tunnels and passages lead to a dead end," she finishes before we take the right that opens into the larger tunnel.

"I guess I'll just have to see it all for myself. I am glad I have you to show me the ways," I reply.

It looks like we've just entered an abandon subway without the tracks. The tunnel is very well built, in a perfect arch from bottom to top, with what looks to be concrete blocks, with electrical wires wrapped in conduit runs along the walls, and lights that are lit here and there along the way. I'm surprised from the looks of them that they even work at all. I mean, who would be responsible for changing the bulbs down here anyway? I'm sure once the others took over under here, the city pretty much forgot about it, and leaves it for them to do with as they may. A few open places from the street above, that look to be drainage spillways for rainwater, are how most of the path is lit. There's a trench along the sides for the water to run off. Thank God today is warmer than yesterday. However, there are still a few patches of ice here and there. We have to be careful not to slip.

"We should be getting close now, Austin," she says after we've been walking for at least an hour.

I hear voices getting louder as we walk closer to another opening. The tunnel opens up into a wide space, with cobblestone lining the path running from left to right. In front of us is what I think to be one of the bars Haley mentioned earlier. It's still somewhat of a tunnel, with higher ceilings, and the walls are square in this part.

I see bodies moving from place to place, walking the streets, in and out of bars. I'm not sure who's human and who's vampire. A couple have had their fangs visible as they've passed. I can tell they know I'm the new guy, because I keep getting weird stares, and it may be creeping me out just a bit.

"Haley, how much farther before we get to your family's lair? The way everyone's looking at me is freaking me out a little."

"Should only be a few more blocks, and you have nothing to worry about as long as you are with me. Everyone knows who I am, and who my father is. He'll have them all burned at the stake if they fuck with me. He's the leader of the coven here in Shreveport. The only power higher than him are the Elders," Haley assures me.

"So, he's the Vampire King of Shreveport?" I ask her.

"Pretty much, yes," she says, placing her hand over her mouth to hide her smile.

Her eyes have even more of a spark to them down here. They seem to be getting bluer the closer we get. I'm starting to think it has something to do with affection that makes her eyes change to such a brilliant shade of blue. Maybe I'm just hoping that when she touched me, she felt some sort of affection. Maybe all these thoughts are just in my head and there really isn't anything to it. Maybe the feeling I get when she looks at me and touches me, are just me being horny and hoping there's more to it because of what I feel for her.

We walk past several more businesses. I hear people moaning and screaming, but not a scared kind of scream. They're screams of pleasure. *Wow*. This is like a soundtrack from a porno, and it's getting louder. As we get closer, there's a weird alleyway running between the business, and another opening crosses the way in front of us.

"Is this normal down here, people just having sex in the streets?" I ask.

"It's pretty normal, yeah. I said they didn't like to feed in the streets. I never said they didn't like to fuck in the streets. Sex is a very open and free thing in the Other World, Austin. Not much is frowned upon in our world when it comes to sexuality. I really wish things in the real world could be the way they are in the Other World. Well, other than the rogue s and the vampires feeding on blood part. I don't think humans would enjoy the blood and guts part of our world. You've been a trooper with all the craziness I've thrown at you. You have to now prepare yourself for more," Haley tells me as we step onto the new path and take a right toward a long string of small doors lining the way. They all have tiny windows with bars covering them in the middle.

"Are these all lairs, Haley? Do we call them that or do we call the dens? I've heard you say both."

"They're known as both—we call ours a lair. Some call their places a den. There's no right or wrong. My parents' lair is just ahead on the right," she tells me as we walk up to the lair—the only one with a porch of sorts in front of it. The door is a nasty black color, and looks like tar.

Haley puts her hand between the bars on the little window and knocks. The door cracks open and this huge guy is standing on the other side, looking like a modern-day Fabio, with long black hair. All I can do is stare.

"Austin, this is my dad. Angelus," she says. Then a beautiful lady steps out from behind him. I can see where Haley gets her looks. "This is my mother, Celina," Haley continues, looking at me as if I'm supposed to do something.

I cough under my breath and reach my hand out to her dad, and damn, his hand grips like a vise. Mine looks small in comparison. Then I shake her mom's hand before we're invited inside.

Walking into a vampire's lair wasn't something a human does every day. A strange feeling washes over me as the door creaks shut behind us, and even though I know I need to go inside so I can get answers, I can't help but wonder what the hell I'm doing.

Chapter 14
HALEY

W e finally make it to my parents' house, and here I am, standing on the porch with a guy who I called a prick just hours ago. He could still be a prick for all I know, but he's been nothing but a true southern gentleman around me. I reach to knock on the door, glancing over at Austin. He always looks so nervous. Hopefully once we get him some answers and get those Thompson boys off his back, he will get to relax a little, but probably not anytime soon.

My dad answers the door and Austin's jaw pretty much drops as he looks up at him. It's a normal thing when people meet my dad. It's not every day you meet someone as big as he is, with such long hair. My mom walks out shortly after my dad and I introduce my parents to him and then we all go inside.

Jonah is sitting at the bar holding a wine glass filled with red liquid.

"Is that what I think it is in his glass, Haley?" Austin whispers to me.

I can't help but laugh. "No, Austin, it's punch or Kool-Aid, I'm sure. Hell, it could even be wine, but he isn't feeding yet, so it's not blood. He's still dhampir and has so far still leaned toward his human side. My mom has to go above-ground a couple days a month to buy groceries for him."

"Oh Haley, he'll learn all of this soon enough. I can't

imagine how crazy all of this must be for you, Austin," my mom says before leading us over to sit on the only sofa in the house.

My parents hardly sit in here, and when they do, they sit at the bar stools where Jonah is now, around the bar. Vampires are restless creatures by habit, other than when they're sleeping, and even then, they still dream just as they did when they were human. The vampire mind never rests.

The lair consists of the room we're in now, with a very small kitchen and the bar to separate the two. Just off the kitchen is a door that goes into my brother's room, which is like any normal human bedroom. Another room inside the door next to his is where my old room used to be. There's still a bed in there, but all of my things are at my apartment. The door on the other side of the living area goes into my parents' sleeping quarters. I've only been allowed in there maybe twice my whole life. I freaked out the first time I walked in to see caskets on each side of the room, with a large bed in the middle. Needless to say, I didn't ask them why they needed a bed if they sleep in the caskets. I think we can all figure that one out.

Yeah. Enough about that.

"Dad, what's your plan to get Austin in front of the Elders?" I ask him.

"We need to be leaving here soon. It'll take us at least an hour to get there. I could flash there faster, but that's not going to get Austin there any faster," Dad replies.

This is true, his human body couldn't handle the force from the speed during the flash. Now that I think about it, I'm not sure if my body would be able to handle it, either. Even being half vampire, I don't have the healing powers my parents have to handle that kind of speed. I'm not sure if

Jonah does or not, but that will all be found out when the time comes.

"What do we need to do to prepare for our trip—or, should I say, to prepare him to go before the Elders?" I ask.

"Oh, this is going to be good," my brother chimes in.

"You should probably go to your room, seeing as this has nothing to do with you," my dad tells him.

Seeing Jonah and I together, you would never know we were brother and sister. He has Dad's jet-black hair and brown eyes. He was slender like me up until about a year ago, when he started working out and put on some muscle.

He gets up from his seat at the bar and lets out a huff. "It'll be my business if I have to help you protect them!" he mumbles as he slams his bedroom door. I'm sure my dad can handle those guys on his own, but Jonah always says he's my protector. He doesn't handle not being able to do that well.

"Haley, there really isn't anything we can do to prepare him. He needs to tell them everything he can about what he remembers of his parents and what the Thompson boys have been doing to you two. The Elders will most likely want to keep you two here so you can be protected," Dad explains.

"But sir, I can't stay here. I have to work. I already only work two days a week. I can't miss those days," Austin says.

"Son, from what Haley has told us, you don't have a place to stay, and you won't be safe at the shelter. I can tell you that if they get their hands on you, it won't be good, and without anyone there to help you, there's no way you can fight them off. Not even a professional MMA fighter could take on the strength of three vampires. Hell, not even a team of professional fighters could have enough strength to compete with those guys. You'll stay here. I will not have my daughter or you in danger. Understood?" Angelus says.

"Yes, sir."

"Good. I'll have Celina call your work and take care of things. If they don't understand, I know plenty of people in the city and will find you another job. First, though, we have more pressing matters to take care of." Dad's voice seems to be getting deeper with every word he speaks.

I grab Austin by the hand and assure him that everything is going to be okay, and that my family will do anything they can to help him. Once I have my fingers locked onto his, I realized I was holding his hand like we've been dating for months. It felt right—like I was supposed to be here.

The tingle, the spark between us when we touch. It feels like this is where I'm supposed to be, where I'm meant to be. Like I've always been here. We lock eyes and my knees get weak. I feel like I'm going to pass out. Suddenly I feel my mom take my hand and pull it away from his.

"You two have no idea what's going on here, do you?" Mom asks.

Chapter 15
AUSTIN

Here I am, standing in the lair of the darkest, largest man I have ever met in my life.

He's informed me that I'll be staying in the depths of the city until we can figure out what's going to happen with the Thompsons and myself. He says they won't give up until they've captured me, and that I need to be protected. That this was the safest place for me, for now.

I should be nervous and worried for my life at this point, but I'm not. It feels like this is where I belong, where I'm meant to be. Standing next to the most beautiful woman I've ever seen, in the living room of the vampire king and his wife. It's as if I've always been here. I have to admit that the streets, tunnels, passageways—whatever you call it outside this door—did kind of leave me feeling uneasy, but not in here. Not with Haley and her family.

Why does it feel like I'm home? I don't know these people at all, but I don't feel like this is my first time here.

"Let's get moving, the Elders are expecting us. Austin, remember to tell them anything you remember before your parents died, what the investigation turned up after their death, and the damage the guys did to your vehicle. It'll feel as if you're going before a court of law. They will ask you many questions," Haley's mom tells me.

They inform Jonah that we are leaving and make him lock and bolt the door behind us. We get out on the path and as soon as we do, Haley stops. It's almost as if she stopped breathing for a moment.

"It's your parents Austin, this is the last time I'll hear them. They said you're safe now. You will see the future soon. Find your destiny, son. Your dad says they can go peacefully into the other side now, but know they are never far away," she tells me.

This is the point when I should break down and cry, but it feels like a strength has come over me. My blood feels like it's rushing through my body, I feel a rush burning through my muscles, and fire in my throat. "What's happening to me?"

"Austin, your eyes just changed colors three times. I've never seen anything like this before," Haley says.

"Oh, my child I've seen this. We have to get to the Elders and we have to get there quickly. Austin, you're going to feel some pains for the next few hours. It's only going to get worse before it gets better. Haley, stay close to him and keep your hand on him. He needs your power," Celina says

"Mom, what's wrong with him, is he going to be okay? I'm supposed to be protecting him. What's my power? Wait! I *have* a power?" Haley asked.

"Haley, for now you just need to keep your hands on him. That's your power—staying strong for him," her mom replies.

BUT THAT DIDN'T LAST LONG.

I can't tell at this point if I'm getting stronger or weaker. It's hard to stand on my feet when I feel like I'm floating. My jaw feels like it's stretching, and my face is on fire. "Mrs. Devile, what's happening to me? Am I dying? Is this why my parents left, are they taking me to the other side with them?" I ask her as I wrap my arm around Haley.

"You're dying in a sense, but you will live forever," Angelus tells me.

Then I black out, for what seemed like hours. When I woke, I was being carried by him. The man just told me I was dying and now he's carrying me? Am I already dead? Is this just my spirit looking back at me? I tried to speak, but the words come out faint.

"Did I die?" I ask, finding the strength to look up.

"You'll have to go through that pain a few more times Austin, this is just the beginning," Celina says.

I feel like I've slept for hours. I look turn my head to the right and I'm staring Angelus in the face. "I think I can stand now; I feel like I have my strength back," I tell him as he pretty much drops me from his arms. Thankfully my strength has returned and I don't fall.

When I finally gain my ground to stand, we're in front of a huge structure that's been carved into the stone, with large columns across the front. It looks like a courthouse you would see on TV, only it's a little more ornate. Just like with the lairs, there are no windows. Large double doors stand in the middle. We walk up to the door and Mr. Devile grabs the copper snake shaped handles and opens the door.

When the door opens, the inside is breathtaking. Even more ornate than the outside are the details in this hallway. Shiny marble floors, paintings and statues line the way. It's at least fifteen feet before we reach another set of doors, and these aren't quite as tall as the ones before. Celina and Angelus each grab a handle to open both doors at the same time.

We enter a large chamber with marble benches in half a

circle pattern from front to back, and the floors and walls are also covered in marble. At the front of the chamber is a large marble podium. I think we would call it the judge's bench in my regular world. Soon after entering, the voice of a women speaks.

"You finally made it. Bring him forward. I was only able to see him once before he was taken away from us."

What does she mean by saying before he was taken from us? I have to wonder if she's talking about me. Angelus and Celina take seats in the first row and they nod for Haley and I to go forward toward the bench.

As we approach, an older woman maybe in her sixties rises from her seat behind the podium. Beautiful grey hair flanks her face, and she has skin which is the color of caramel. Her eyes are just as icy blue as Haley's. In her right hand, she holds a staff covered in beautiful jewels.

"Oh, Austin, my child. I see you have begun your change," she speaks.

Haley pushes me forward and takes a step back to sit with her parents. Standing before her, I feel like I'm being judged but I've done nothing wrong.

"What do you mean, I have begun my change?" I ask her.

"I'll explain it all when the Elders enter the room, Austin. I have to be sure to leave out no parts."

Another short black-haired lady soon enters the room from the door to the left.

"Eva Davenport," the grey-haired lady announces.

Soon following her were two guys who look almost the same, one maybe older than the other. They were both bald with beards and the same golden eyes as the lady who entered before them.

to let you know they're still after Austin, and they aren't giving up on finding him."

"Thank you, Stacy. It's late, so I think we'll be safe here for the night, but we'll get up and leave here as early as possible in the morning."

"I just thought you would want to know. Call me with any updates tomorrow, and I'll also let you know if I see those assholes around anywhere. Rob locked the car inside the shop for the night so they won't be able to get to it. You two be careful. Goodnight," Stacy says with a worried tone to her voice.

"Goodnight and I will keep in touch!" I tell her, hanging up the phone.

I look over at Austin and let him know what Stay had to say. No sooner than I could get the words out, I hear, "I told you, we don't have much time," from Austin's dad.

Then I start to freak out. His parents have followed us the whole time. I sure as hell hope they didn't see what I did in my room earlier. I don't know how that works, I can only hear them. I don't see them so maybe—hopefully—they can't see me either.

I can tell Austin is worried, but he isn't letting me know. Hell, I'm a little worried myself.

As much as I would love to sit here and look at his fine ass all night, I know I have to get to bed. His clothes have already been in the dryer for an hour so they should be done.

Once he's changed back into his clothes, he comes back to sit on the sofa, closer to me this time. The tiny hairs on my arms stand at attention. He's like static electricity every time he's near me, and I have to stand up to have a reason to move away.

"Jareth and Drake Davenport."

"I would like for you all to meet my grandson Austin Johnson," the lady announces. "Austin, I'm Athena. Your grandmother."

My face feels frozen. I want to speak, but the words won't come out. This lady just called me her grandson. How is this possible? I thought my grandmother was dead. My father took me to her grave.

This must be a dream. *It has to be*. I have to be stuck in a dream.

"Come closer, Austin," the shorter lady tells me.

"Bring Haley with you," her brother speaks up.

Haley looks to both of her parents for the okay to come forward, first to her father, and then to her mother, and I watch as they both nod with agreement.

She joins me as we step up onto a small step just in front of where the Elders now sit. The lady who calls her herself my grandmother stands beside them to the right of the bench. The sister sits in the middle, with a brother on each side.

"AUSTIN, YOU MUST LISTEN AND LISTEN CAREFULLY. WE WERE hoping this wouldn't happen until after you met with us and we had taken care of your problems with those asshole brothers," the man on the right says.

"You have been lied to. Your whole life is a lie. As harsh as this may sound, it's the truth," the man continued.

Followed by the sister. "Your father was a vampire, Austin. He went on the run with you and your mom when you were eight. Am I right?" She looks to the grey-haired lady.

"You were seven, Austin. You turned eight a few months after you guys left New Orleans. I searched for you, but somehow, he disguised the scent every time I would get close," the lady said.

"But my father told me you were dead."

"Your father always rebelled against me, Austin. Once he turned from dhampir to full vampire, there was nothing more I could do or say to change his ways. He went rogue for a while before meeting your mother. Once he met her and they had you, he decided to hunt and kill his own kind, dragging you and your mother along with him."

"You were always left with a friend or a neighbor, or so I am told, while they went out to do their deeds. The grave you visited was my mother's grave, your great grandmother. I am sorry you're just hearing all of this now, but it's finally time, now that your father is no longer here to cover the lies. You too are a dhampir, Austin. And I'm afraid to tell you this, but you being around Haley has set your testosterone into overdrive. You've started your change into vampire," the old lady tells me.

I turn to run after that. All I want to do is leave this place and never look back. My head is spinning from all the information, and I can't process it as panic overwhelms me.

I just can't be in this room anymore.

Chapter 16
HALEY

I watched as Austin's face froze in a mask of fear. A moment later, he turns and bolts out of the room. My first instinct is to follow him, and I start to until one of the Elders speaks up.

"Let him go, he'll be back shortly. He has nowhere to run, and besides, he has no idea where he's going," Drake tells me as he walks back to take his seat on the bench. Looking over to his sister, he says, "Now tell her what's really going on and why she's here."

As Eva hesitates, looking like she's searching for words, I think back on what happened on the way to the chambers. When Austin put his arm around me, his eyes turned green, ice blue, and then grey. He started shivering and asked if he was dying. I knew what was happening once he started shivering, but I played it off and told him I've never seen this before.

Just about the time I realized what was going on, my father speaks up. "You're dying in a sense, but you will live forever."

As he passed out, Dad swooped him up into his arms and carried him the rest of the way. He walked at least another four blocks with Austin in his arms. No sooner then we approached the chambers, Austin's head popped up as if nothing happened, and he fell from my father's arms and stumbled to his feet.

When we entered the chambers, we were met with a beautiful older lady who claimed to be Austin's grandmother, and then the Elders entered the room, calling me to join Austin at the bench. I had no idea what any of this had to do with me or why I was called before the Elders. I knew they would question me, but I didn't think it would be before speaking with him first.

They began to tell Austin his whole life story, and that this lady was really in fact his grandmother. They were pretty much saying his father lied to him his whole life.

Eva stands from her seat, bringing me back to the present, the look on her face saying she found the words she searched for. "Haley, have you two noticed anything strange when you get close to each other? Like a spark, maybe a source of energy that ignites between the two of you when you touch. Your eye color may become clearer or even appear to be darker. Have any of these things happened over the past few days?"

"We think you two are fated, bonded mates destined to be together from birth. It's been shown in all of the card readings I've done, and seeing that Austin has started his change before death just proves that it's fate. You being his one true mate has caused him to change. Other than death, it's the only way one can go from dhampir to vampire."

His grandmother comes down to stand in front of me and places her staff upon my forehead. "You are gifted, child. You can hear things from the other side, but you can't see the things that are happening right before your eyes."

I have no idea what to do at this point. Austin has left me standing here, taking all of this in on my own, and my parents are just sitting there like none of this is even happening. Do they not even give a shit that I was just told I was the true mate of a guy I just met yesterday? *Wow*, this isn't shocking news at all for them. Is this why they sent me away from the city?

I feel as if they have been keeping a lie from me, and now I want to run out of the room myself. But in the end, I decide that staying here is maybe for the best. Maybe having a mate isn't a bad thing. Having someone to share my life with, someone to share the empty apartment—it can only enhance my life. I can't see it taking anything away from it.

And what I knew of Austin so far told me he was a good guy. So, no—I wasn't going to run just. Not yet, anyway.

"If I'm his one true mate and that's the reason for his change, then why am I not changing?" I ask, confused.

"It's not the same for all dhampir kind, Haley. You can feel his power and his energy. That's how you know you're his mate. The only person who can feel the energy of another is that person's only true mate. The force between the two will only get stronger, and the bonds will not be broken—even if this love between the two of you has been tainted by his father. The Devile and Johnson families have never seen eye to eye, but fate has chosen otherwise," Drake says as he stands.

"Well, look who decided to come back and join us," Jareth said as he also stood, joining his brother as they walked to greet Austin, who just came back into the room after being gone for about twenty minutes.

"Come join us, Austin," Drake says as his sister comes to stand just in front of me, joined by Austin's grandmother.

"Take her hand Austin, and turn to face her," the older lady says.

The moment he touches fingers, I feel a bolt of energy as his power source raged through me. I look into his eyes and they're the most amazing shade of blueish grey that I've ever seen. The hair on my arms stands on its end, and I'm left without words. Speechless felt like an understatement in that moment.

"You see that, Haley? You feel it? That's how you know he's your one true mate. The one thing your parents tried to protect you from by removing you from the Other World. Yes! Another daywalker whose vampire laid dormant until this day. The day his one fated mate changed his life forever," Eva tells me.

The Elder brothers each put a hand on mine and Austin's shoulders, pulling us apart.

"The two of you must try avoid any further contact until Austin's change is complete, and then you two must mate. The mating of one's true mate causes the unbreakable bond to be complete. This bond will be the only way Austin will ever be safe and no longer in danger from the brothers," Eva tells us.

My father then steps forward and places his hand on my forehead. "This isn't what I wanted for my daughter. I wanted you to have a life outside the Other World. To live freely in the world above. Not to be fated to some homeless kid living in the streets," he says, looking over at Austin with a smirk on his face. "But after meeting this guy, I knew nothing could change what has to be. It's fate, and your mother and I knew it was happening days before you came to tell us he was the one. You have my blessing. You two will stay with us until we're sure Austin has completed his change." He finished talking about the same time Jareth starts to speak.

"We'll find the Thompsons and deal with them accordingly, but I'm sure if they know you two have been to see us, they'll be on the run for a few days. We know their routine all too well. You should take Austin back to the lair now and let him rest. The days ahead will be hell for him."

Austin's grandmother steps up to me, once again placing her staff on my forehead.

"You take care of him, my child. I have great things waiting for the two of you. And you'll need me once Austin shares his full energy with you. Your powers will become unbearable. I'll be the one to help you control them," she tells me, removing her staff. She steps over and places the staff just the same on his forehead.

I turn to see Austin's face frozen with every little expression, making me realize he hasn't said a word. He is literally speechless.

"This is your fate, son, and so it shall be done."

Chapter 17

AUSTIN

R unning from the chamber most likely wasn't the best way for me to handle things, but it was just too much for me to take in all at once. Hearing that my father had lied to me for so many years. Suddenly finding out that my grandmother is still alive, and the little fact of, *Oh, you're becoming a vampire Austin, it's no big deal.*

Yeah, that might be just a little too much for me to take in. After sitting outside the chamber for twenty minutes, I have to go back in and face the music. Running from it isn't going to solve anything. Just before I open the door, I hear Eva speaking to Haley.

"Haley, have you two noticed anything strange when you get close to each other? Like a spark, maybe a source of energy that ignites between the two of you when you touch. Your eye color may become clearer or even appear to be darker. Have any of these things happened over the past few days?"

"We think that you two are fated, bonded mates destined to be together from birth. It's been shown in all of the card readings I've done, and seeing that Austin has started his change before death just proves that it's fate. You being his one true mate has caused him to change. Other than death, it's the only way one can go from dhampir to vampire."

This is like being suddenly married in the human. world. Vampires think this is normal, while I on the other hand may be a little taken aback with all this—okay, a *lot* taken aback. But I have these feeling for her that I cannot explain, and deep in my soul I know everything they are saying is true.

Maybe a little weird, but true. And, strangely enough, I don't mind the idea of being mated to Haley at all.

When I walk into the chamber, the older woman was standing before Haley with her staff upon her forehead. "You are gifted, child. You can hear things from the other side, but you can't see the things that are happening right before your eyes."

Inhaling deeply, I walk up to join Haley in front of the beach. I'm greeted by the Elder brothers, telling me to come join them, as their sister takes her place in front of Haley and I.

"Take her hand, Austin."

Once I touch just the tips of her fingers, I can feel my energy leaving my body. It's the same as before when we touched, but this time it's even stronger. Once I'm holding her hand and our fingers are locked, she has my full strength. I can feel her life force surging through my veins. Her eyes, once blue, have now turned grey. They're cold and still like ice. The need to fuck her overcame me. I felt a light in my eyes, and just when I got lost in her eyes—

The two brothers grab our hands, one Haley's and one mine, pulling us apart. Once my hand left hers, I felt like part of me was gone. Like I had given part of myself to her. It was the feeling of emptiness.

"You two must try not make any contact until Austin has completed his change," Drake speaks.

Those were not the words I wanted to hear after what I just felt from touching her. But telling us to wait for my change and then we must mate to complete the bond between us sounded great to me. It kind of felt like I mated with her just from touching her hand. I can't imagine how it's going to be once we bond.

Wait, why am I talking as if this is normal? I'm about to become a vampire, and just got fated to mate and bond with a girl that I only just met. But like I thought before, it just felt *right*, as strange as that sounded.

Her dad gives her a speech about how he didn't see his daughter being the one true mate of a homeless guy, and it really has me standing here feeling not so good about myself—until he looked over at me with a half ass grin on his face, making it clear he'd been teasing. "After meeting Austin, I knew nothing could break the bonds between you two, and you have my blessing," he tells Haley.

Thankfully, because the last thing I want to do is get a vampire lord on my bad side—not today or any other day, for that matter.

I really need to have a talk with my grandmother at some point, but she seems in a hurry to go after she tells Haley to take care of me, and that she will need her when I've given her my full energy source. I shouldn't be thinking dirty with my grandmother standing next to her, but all I can think of is, *I will give her my full energy source, all right.*

The staff in her hand then comes down upon my forehead, breaking me from my thoughts.

"This is your fate, son, and so it shall be done," she tells me as she turns to leave the room. I start to speak, but she stops me before I can get a word out. "Austin, it will all come to you. We have many things to discuss, but now isn't the place or the time to do so. I'm sure the Elders have had enough of us for one day. Now, you go with these fine people and get some rest. You'll need it for the hell you are about to endure. For now, I shall leave you be."

She closes the door behind her as she leaves the room. The Elders leave the bench to follower her, but not before Eva turns to say, "We will be seeing you again real soon."

Once they have all left the room, I turn to look at Haley and she looks just as shocked as I am.

"What the hell just happened?" I ask.

Haley's mom comes up behind me and puts her hand on my shoulder. "It seems that what we knew all along has happened. The two of you are mates, and there's nothing we can do to change it."

Suddenly, I can feel the cold of the marble beneath my feet. It's so cold, my feet start to sting, and it's rising up my legs and now into my waist. All the heat from my body feels as if it's leaving me. Shivering, I fall to my knees and wrap my arms around myself. The words come between chattering teeth. "Haley, I need you. I need to feel you. Please warm me."

I try to continue speaking but the words don't come. And then the world goes dark.

"Come sit for a while, Austin," I hear a female voice say. My eyes open and it's my mother, sitting on a tree stump next to a creek. "You're safe here; the change is upon you. It won't be long now. You must know I had nothing to do with your father's decisions. I just wanted to protect you, and he died trying to hide the truth from you," she says, just before my eyes closed and the world went black once again.

"Austin, Austin, Austin!" I feel my body shaking and the voice of an angel calling my name. Then a slight tap on my cheek causes my eyes to open once more. It's Haley, wearing dark colored mitten looking things on her hands, shaking me and tapping my face. "You had another black out Austin, are you getting weaker?"

I was by no means getting weaker. If anything, I was getting stronger. I could see colors so strongly; it was as if I could feel them. The shirt Haley's wearing is so brown, I can see the orange tones peeping through. The white of the room now shines as if a light has been lit behind it. The tap of her gloved hand feels like it's pushing into my face. I can smell the coconut from the shampoo she used to wash her hair. The perfume of the ladies who just left the room. The copper smell of blood envelopes my nose.

"Holy fuck, my senses have been sent into hyperdrive. This is unbelievable. I'm not sure this is a good thing. Will this be how it is for the rest of my life?" I ask Celina as I pick myself up from the floor.

"It will be, yes, but you will learn to control it. You will learn to control many things. The most important is your thirst for blood. That has to be at the top of your list of things to learn to control. It can be dangerous in many ways if you don't. Now, let's get you back to the lair, so you can get that rest your grandmother says you need," she replies as she puts her hand on my back to turn me in the other direction.

We walked back out of the tall double doors, and I marveled at them. I had no idea how big they really were when we came in before. They stand at least ten feet tall. Walking out into the passageway, I can now see the parts I missed while I was being carried. This part of the Other World looks much different than that of the area with the lairs. It's much wider here, more like a street. They have no cars, bikes, or trains down here. They don't need them. They have the ability to flash from one place to another. No transport needed when your body can move at super speeds, I suppose.

I'm surprised at how well maintained everything is. Cobblestone streets even pave the way. Nothing like the concrete and dirt over near the bookstore. You could tell they took pride in keeping it nice around the chambers. I think we've walked a mile when the path starts to narrow, and it gets a bit darker. I feel my eyes get wider and adjust to the darkness, making it as bright as the light we just left. The stones beneath our feet become fewer the farther we walk.

"Is this the way we came before?" I ask.

"It is, Austin. You were blacked out, remember? It will become darker as we go from one passage to the next, for about five blocks or so. Then we'll be back to the place we were right before your change started," Haley replies.

She was right, it became completely dark with no light source of any kind. Yet I could still see. I could see just as well in the darkness as I could in the daylight above. My sense of smell seems to be even stronger in the dark as well. I can smell the blood, so much I can practically taste it. I *crave* it. Then I hear the voice of a female being taken sexually by someone. They're fucking against the wall just as we passed, and I then realize it's her blood I smell. The sweet coppery smell washes over me, and I want to push him out of the way and taste her for myself.

This isn't right, control yourself. Austin, I think to myself. *Haley is my mate and I'd hoped her blood to be the first blood I taste.*

But that's not all I want to taste. I want to taste *her*. I want taste every part of her body, of course spending as much time between those thighs as I can. I can't wait to make this woman my mate. It's fated, so it must be done.

The fucked-up part is having to wait. Some shit about if we choose to mate before I change, it could fuck up our bonds, was what the Elders told us. I think waiting to fuck her will be harder for me to control than my thirst for blood is going to be. My dick, whether it should be or not, is rock hard just thinking about it.

I have made sure to keep myself in front of them so they don't notice. Hopefully before we get back into the light, it will have gone down.

The change is upon you, it won't be long now, keeps repeating over and over in my head. I'm craving blood, the taste of raw flesh beneath my tongue. How the hell did I become one of the not so lucky ones to be changed before my death?

I'm so pissed at my parents for hiding this from me my whole life, and I have to find out from a bunch of strangers. A vampire was damn sure not on my list of things I wanted to be when I grew up.

Chapter 18
HALEY

O nce Austin falls to the floor with another blackout, I can feel my energy being drained from me. It feels like my life source is being pulled from me. I move to put my hands on him, to hold him, to take away his pain. Just as I go to put my hands on him, my mother pulls me back.

"You can't touch him yet, Haley," she says as she pulls a pair of mittens from her purse. "Put these on before you touch him."

Putting these things on feels weird as hell, but I do it, even though I'm afraid to try to touch him now, even with the mittens on. I reach to shake his shoulder first and call his name. When that doesn't work, I poke him in the face with my mitten covered fingers, finally causing his eyes to open.

This time the grey had taken over. His eyes have gone cold. Not in a bad way, but in the most beautiful way possible. So beautiful they draw me in, and it's all I can do to control myself from leaning in and taking him right then and there.

Good thing my parents are here, or the bond would be broken already. I have to learn to keep myself under control until Austin has made his change. The more he changes toward his vampire side, the more I'm drawn to him. And once he's off the floor, I can still feel his energy, even though we aren't touching.

The walk back home is long. Austin seems to be a new person, pointing out every little detail in the pathways. Even when we reach the darkest point, he still seems to see as clear as day. He also seems to know where he's going and stays in front of my parents and I for most of the walk.

"This has been a crazy, long ass day, and I'm so happy to be back here at the lair," I say as my dad reaches to unlock the door.

My brother greats us on the other side. "The Thompson brothers came by earlier, beating on the door. They were asking me where your boyfriend was, Haley. They also called you my fine ass sister. They must need glasses."

"No time for you to be a smart-ass, Jonah. What did you tell them?" I ask.

"Well, I told them I have no idea who the Austin guy was that they were asking about, and that my parents weren't home. They also said that they would kill you and anyone else that stood in their way of getting to Austin," my little brother says right before our father speaks up.

"I will stand in their fucking way, and I dare them to lay a hand on any member of this family, Austin included."

I stand in awe of what's going on before me. How the fuck did I just meet this guy, and then suddenly, today I'm his mate, and my father just instantly made him part of our family?

"So, you guys don't find it odd at all that two days ago I was your single daughter and today I'm being forced on someone as his mate?" I ask my parents. I probably should have thought that through a little before saying it in front of Austin—but it's crazy that my parents are just playing it off as if it was a normal thing. As if Austin and I had been married for years, and not even speaking of the fact that I must mate with him after only knowing him for a few days.

"Haley, in the human world this would not be normal at all, but here in the Other World, *our* world, it's how things happen. You and Austin have been fated as mates since birth. As weird as it sounds, it's meant to be and it *shall* be. It's what some would say has been written in the stars." Mother always seems to have the right words for everything.

I push Jonah out of my way and walk over to sit on the couch. Austin comes to sit down next to me, but he pauses when I remind him that he can't make contact, and he walks over to take a seat at the bar.

"My parents don't have a television in here, but if you get bored, Jonah streams live TV in his room," I tell Austin.

"Oh, that's just great. Pawn your vampire boyfriend off on your little brother—who's still human. Did you forget that, Haley? That vampires still like to feed on us humans?" Jonah laughs, waving his hand in my face.

"You're so dumb, Jonah! You know you're not human by any means, and besides, who would want your nasty blood?" I tell him as he turns to walk to his room. He is so the typical little brother.

"Austin, it looks like you get to sleep on a couch two nights in row. I'm not sure how comfortable you'll be here, but still, it's got to be better than your cold ass car. Speaking of, we need to contact Rob about your car, and Stacy as well, to let her know what's going on. My phone has no service down here, so when we go back to get some clothes and things, we can call them then," I tell him.

"It isn't safe for us to leave here until morning, Haley. Something tells me that danger is waiting on us just outside that door. I can sense it," Austin replies, putting his face in his hands and rubbing his forehead. "When I blacked out in the chamber, I saw my mother, Haley. She told me that it wouldn't be long and that I was safe now," he continued.

I don't know what to say to him. I just wish I could hold him in my arms for comfort, to kiss him, to feel his emotions. "You're right, Austin. We can wait till morning. And that's normal—you will now have premonitions about things from here on out. Now, you should get some rest."

AUSTIN

Everyone has gone to bed, leaving me here on the couch. I could have gone into Jonah's room to watch television, but I decided to stay in here, in this dark room. Quietness over takes my thoughts, and my childhood flashes before me. The more I remember, the more nothing about my life seems normal. I guess this would explain why my mother's side of the family wanted nothing to do with my father or myself. But why would my mom tell her parents she was married to a vampire?

I turn on my stomach and drop my hand to the concrete floor beside the couch and start tracing the marks scratched into it. My finger begins to move faster and faster, and soon they're moving faster than my eyes can follow. *Whoa*. I grab it with my other hand to make it stop and move my head closer to the edge, so I can get a better look.

Not having any control of the motion my hand was making, I had drawn a logo of some sorts into the floor. I feel no pain in my hand or fingers at all, from the burn I have caused in the concrete floor before me. Curiosity flows through me, and I'm sure the others know what this is, but I'm not about to walk into a room with caskets filled with sleeping vampires.

And if I go into the room with Haley, I'm sure I won't be able to keep myself from crawling in her bed and having my way with her. As a matter of fact, I *know* I won't be able to control myself if I go in there. My desire to mate rises with every hour of this change. I want to taste blood so bad it's driving me mad. The craving is deep within my soul to drink and, most importantly, to take my mate, to claim her.

What the fuck is happening to me? I have had sex; I have wanted to fuck girls before. This was not the same. I can't shut it off, I can't stop my dick from getting hard—I can't stop the urge to mate, or the thirst for blood.

I can't let myself be overtaken by the darkness. I've read this shit in books, and I never thought it was real—but this is as real as it gets. How do I know the darkness is not what I crave? I close my eyes, forcing the thoughts from my mind, and I go blank. *Fuck now I can control my thoughts*, was my last thought before drifting off to sleep.

When the morning comes, I'm woken by Jonah in the kitchen, banging pots and pans. I wipe the sleep from my eyes and go sit on the stool at the bar. "What is all that noise for?" I ask him.

"Oh, I'm just making oatmeal. Mom and Dad won't be up for hours, and your little girlfriend will sleep all day if you don't wake her up," the dark-haired kid tells me. I ask him why they would sleep all day, and he replied, "Vampires hunt at night, Austin. My parents sleep during the day and Haley, well, she's just lazy. It could be also that she got used to sleeping all day when she lived here." He laughed as he said the last.

"I guess that makes sense, but she was up before me when I stayed at her house," I tell him.

"You two have nothing better to talk about than me this early in the morning?" Haley asks as she walks into the room.

"I need you two to come look at something," I say as I

walk over to the couch and point at the floor. "I did this without even knowing what I was doing. My hand started moving at super human speed and before I could stop it, this had happened."

They both look at the floor and then back at each other several times before Haley finally speaks. "Austin, that's a coven mark."

"But it isn't our coven's mark," her brother adds.

Haley walks over to the bar, places her hands on the counter, and drops her head as she lets out a sigh before lifting her head to speak again. "It means he isn't part of our coven, Jonah. He has his own, but how is this possible if we are to be mates? It's not known for two covens to get along for even more than a few moments in the same place, much less become mates."

My heart skips a beat—maybe even stops beating at all —hearing her say those words. This has to mean something else. There's no way that we aren't mates. Even the Elders knew we were mates before we had a clue.

"Haley, that can't be the case, you know we were meant to be mates. You feel the same way I do when we touch, when you look into my eyes. We're fated. I don't care what some symbol on the floor tells me. Even if I drew the damn thing with my fingers, you are and will forever be mine." I said the words without even realizing what I was saying.

"Oh, now I'm yours, huh?" Haley smirks.

"Well once we're mated, yes, you'll be mine. But I can already feel it, Haley. I feel like we're bonded. I felt it the very first day." I place my hand on my chest and walk toward her. "Don't you feel it?" I ask.

"Of course, I do Austin, but this symbol on the floor could change all of that. If you're part of a coven that's indeed enemies with my father's coven, we won't be allowed to be together at all. And he damn sure won't allow any mating," she says, walking back to the sofa and looking at the mark on the floor once more, scraping her foot over it.

This can't be happening to me. Just when things are starting to go great in my life—even if this shit is a little weird and yes, I may still be a just a bit freaked out by all of it. But I'm truly sure this is where I'm supposed to be. Right here, with her for a mate.

I walk to stand next to her. I want to reach for her and hold her in my arms. This not being able to touch is really pissing me off, but I'm not going to do anything to fuck up the bond or the mating. "Haley, I feel like this mark was made for me. I felt no evil when it was happening. I did feel like it was not of my control but mentally I was telling my hand what to do. This mark is my own."

I have no idea where those words came from or why I even said them.

This mark is my own.

The room goes black.

Chapter 20
HALEY

When I walk into the living room and see this mark on the floor, I knew something wasn't right about it. I pace the floors from one room to the other, trying to figure out what's going on. I walk back to the spot where Austin says he made the mark—or coven symbol, as we call them in the Other World. He comes to stand beside me, almost reaching out to touch me before I move, making him miss. He starts to speak in a deeper voice than he does normally.

"This mark is my own," he says just before his eyes roll back in his head and he once again blacks-out, falling onto the floor.

I try to catch him, but I remember our fate. The bond could be broken. Jonah isn't standing close enough to grab him before he hits the floor. He at least did not fall hard, and went down slowly, with his head leaning against the couch.

"Jonah, grab the pillow to put under his head," I tell him as he comes walking around the other side of Austin.

He leans down to put the pillow under his head and then he says, "The skin on his neck is ice cold." I tell him to check his arms and hands and he says the same. "They are just as cold."

I'm a little in shock of what's going on and have no idea what I need to do to help him. His eyes are still open, yet still no movement. Before even thinking about what I was doing, I find myself beating on my parents' bedroom door, yelling, "*Help*! Something has happened to Austin. Please come help!"

"They're not here, Haley!" Jonah tells me as his puts his hand on my back and walks me back over to Austin. "Maybe you have to touch him. You're his mate, and maybe, like in fairytales, this shit could work," my brother blurts out.

I don't even think twice about him cussing, it's the Other World, everything goes here. I second guess touching him, though. I get so close, placing my hand just above his chest. Then I remember, I can possibly contact his grandmother telepathically. I mean, it's worth a try. It's something I've never done, but if she can contact me, then there has to be a way I can contact her.

I tell Jonah what I'm doing and for him to not leave Austin, and I go into my old room in complete darkness. I sit on the floor with my legs crossed and place my hands on each side of my head, focusing to bring her into my thoughts. Taking a few deep breaths, I try to reach out to her.

Athena, if you can hear me, Austin's in trouble. I need your help. I try over and over but I hear nothing in return. After sitting and trying until my legs start hurting, I'm giving up, but as I start to standup, I hear her voice.

"I'm here." The voice is very low and I can hardly make out what's being said when she speaks again. "I can hear you. Tell me where you are, Haley."

"I'm at my parents' lair, please come quick. I can hardly hear you. We need your help. Austin has blacked out. If you can hear me, please come quick!" I tell her where the lair is and walk back into the room with Austin. Before I'm even all the way in the room, there's a knock at the door.

Jonah walks over to see who it is, and as soon as the door opens, I see Athena is on the other side. How in the hell did she get here so fast? Then it hit me—vampires can flash from one place to another. I wonder if Austin will be able to do this once his change is complete. Will I be able to flash with him? That would be nice if we could flash to any place in the world at any given moment.

"Come in, Mrs. Johnson," Jonah tells the lady standing outside the door.

"Call me Athena," she replies as she comes in and kneels next to Austin, placing her hand on his chest. "He needs to feed. His complete change is still a few days away. However, he's at the point that he will need blood to survive from this day forward. Help me get him onto the sofa." Athena's voice is very stern.

"So, who feeds him? I'm not about to be someone's breakfast!" Jonah says jokingly.

"It's best that his first taste of blood come from his mate, but the time is not right for that. For now, he'll have to take my blood. He will need to feed again within a few days. His change should be complete by then," Athena tells us as she lifts her arm to her mouth, releases her fangs, and bites down into it. Once the blood starts to flow down her arm, she places it over Austin's mouth. "Drink my child, you must drink the blood to live."

The blood starts dripping into his mouth, and soon after, he lifts his head to drink from her arm. His fangs come into full view just before he bites down into her arm and begins to suck from it. His eyes open to reveal the most amazing blue color I've ever seen as his skin turns pale and his jawline becomes more dominate. I can feel heat coming from his body even though his soul just turned cold.

The old Austin is dying, but a new one is being born. It's like he just changed from a boy into a man right before my eyes, and *fuck*, it's so hot! Once my eyes lock onto his, I forget anyone else is even in the room. I feel a pull toward him, as if he's demanding me to come to him. It feels like he has total control over me—mind, body, and soul. It's all I can do to restrain myself from answering my body's demands, or should I say, Austin's demands.

I break the stare between us as I turn to walk away. As much as I would love to stand here and be by his side, I know it's for the best that I walk away for a moment. Otherwise, my brother and his grandmother are going to have to leave. So, I think it's definitely for the best that I step out of the room for a bit.

But as soon as I take a step forward, I feel something grabbed ahold of me, and then a sudden shock covers my whole body. Like I've been hit with a lightning bolt. I don't really know what that would feel like, but I'm almost sure this is as close as you can get to that feeling. However, this feeling was not a shock that would kill someone. It was more of a shock that brought life into me. I felt every hair on my body stand on end. He was in total control, and this time there was nothing I could do or say that would change the fact.

Finally, after what seemed like thirty minutes—in reality, I'm sure it was only thirty seconds—I manage to find the words to speak. "Austin, I can't move with this hold you have on me." I tell him, trying to play it off as if his power had no effect on me whatsoever.

Stop!

"Haley, I don't want you to move, I don't want you to ever leave my side," he said with what seemed to be an even deeper voice than he had just an hour before. "I know it seems crazy, and I had no idea what anyone meant when they said we were fated. But I feel it now. I can feel your energy. Your power. When you looked into my eyes, I felt weightless. I felt my spirit leave me for a moment when you turned to walk away. You're my spirit, my life, Haley. All of my power belongs to you." Austin finishes wiping the blood from his bottom lip.

This really is a lot for me to take in—hearing him say that I'm his life leaves me speechless. For once in my life, I can't form words to respond. I mean, I just met this guy. Yes, I feel the attraction too, and the power he could have over me once I'm no longer able to control it. Well—that kind of scares me a little.

Okay. Maybe more than a little.

I simply reply, "Austin, you must have hit your head when you fell. You're talking nonsense."

Chapter 21

AUSTIN

I hardly remember falling to the floor when I finally open my eyes to realize I'm drinking blood from my grandmother's wrist. The copper taste pleases my taste buds, and I didn't give a shit how weird it was that it was her blood I was drinking. The more I took in, the more powerful I felt.

Opening my eyes, the first thing I see is the beautiful blonde kneeling at my side—the rest of the room was dark, and she was the light. I felt myself being drawn to her. My energy, my body were waking up because she was there. I felt like I died and she's the angel that brought me back to life, even though I'm still taking the blood from my grandmother's wrist. Haley turned to walk away and I felt like I was dying all over again. My strength, my everything, started fading once she turned away from me and started to walk away.

Stop!

"Haley, I don't want you to move, I don't want you to ever leave my side," I say. My voice seems deeper than I remember, but maybe that's just from drinking blood from another person.

"I know it seems crazy, and I had no idea what anyone meant when they said we were fated. But I feel it now. I can feel your energy. Your power. When you looked into my eyes, I felt weightless. I felt my spirit leave me for a moment when you turned to walk away. You're my spirit, my life,

Haley. All of my power belongs to you," I tell her without even understanding anything I'm saying or why I'm saying it. I just know how I feel and that she's mine. My strength, my life depends on her. Wiping the blood from my bottom lip, I finally get the strength to once again stand up, and I come face to face with the lady who I was drinking from only moments ago. "How did you get here, Grandma, and why was I sucking blood from your wrist?"

"Haley beckoned me telepathically when you fell ill, my child. I flashed here as fast as I could and found you lifeless on the floor, because you needed to feed. Your vampire has started to take control of your mind, body, and soul. You needed blood to survive. You can't feed from Haley until you two are mated, so Jonah and I were the only other choices, and he didn't feel comfortable enough to let you feed from him. I wasn't about to lose you when I just got you back into my life. My grandson, you see I had to do what had to be done in order for you to survive."

This is all happening way too fast. My mind is a constant roller coaster of emotions, thoughts, and what ifs. Just two days ago, I had no idea what I was going to do with my life, or where I would even be within a year from that day. Today, I'm in a lair deep under the city full of tunnels, sucking blood from a lady I've never met, who's suddenly wanting me in her life because she's my grandmother.

That part I have no problem with, but why has she waited until now to show back up in my life? Maybe my father had written her off, but I still think she could have made an effort to let me know she existed. On the other hand, how can I be angry with her when she just saved me from dying—or do vampires really die from not feeding?

Wait I'm a vampire! That's kind of fucking cool, yet it

freaks me the fuck out at the same time. I hate my steaks being the least bit rare and now I'm a bloodsucker... Nope, nothing weird or fucked up about that at all. Just a homeless vampire who met his "mate" because his dead parents spoke to her from the other side. Just a perfect, normal day to everyone around me it seems—but to me, not so much.

"So, I can no longer see the light of day—will I only be able to go into the city, or anywhere else for that matter, at night?" I ask.

"That really depends, Austin. Some dhampir have been able to become daywalkers after they've changed. I wouldn't recommend you doing so until you're stronger and have sealed the bond between you and Haley, though."

As soon as the words left her mouth, a loud bang slammed into the door. Jonah walked over, looking out of the small window at the top of the door.

"It's the Thompson brothers!" he whispers as he runs over to where I'm standing.

"Shit, I thought the Elders were supposed to find and take care of them," Haley says.

"Well, it seems they haven't done so well with capturing them, seeing that they are standing on the other side of the door," I reply wryly.

"*Open the fucking door! I know he's in there, I can smell him,*" one of the brothers yell from outside the door.

"*You have nowhere to hide now, you little half breed,*" another brother shouts.

Any other time, I would have gone into panic mode, but this time I went straight into fight mode. I know Haley told me I couldn't take them all on at once, but the beast lurking inside of me now was thinking something totally different. I know, logically, that I can't fight them all off on my own as well as everyone else in the room can do—but my vampire says otherwise.

I rush to the door and place my hand on the lever, but before I could flip the latch to open it, Haley places her hand on top of mine. The power that rushes through me as soon as her hand touches mine is fucking unbelievable. This wasn't supposed to happen. She isn't supposed to be touching me until we've mated. I guess out of fear of me opening the brothers and letting them into her parents' home, she felt it was the only way to stop me from doing something I knew I shouldn't be doing in the first place. The energy that ran through my body was almost overpowering.

Seconds after Haley grabbed my hand, my grandmother came up behind me, placing a hand on my shoulder and the other on Haley's hand to remove it from mine. The grip she had on my hand was not a light one, and Athena had to pry us apart, forcing Haley to let go and move away from me as she came to stand between us.

"Haley, take your brother into the other room. Try to contact your parents to let them know what's going on, and I'll flash to find the Elders. We have to put a stop to this right away. Austin, stay as far away from that door as possible," Athena tells us before she flashes out of the room.

I join Haley and Jonah in his room, closing the door behind me. I wish I knew why these guys were even after me. Why punish me for the things my father did? I was clueless to all of this, after all.

"Haley, maybe if we just talked to them. Maybe if they knew I had no idea about my folks being who they were, maybe they will just leave us alone," I say as I sit down on the bed beside her, being sure not to let our bodies touch.

"Austin, you don't get it. It's in your blood; your bloodline is tainted. You may not be like the rest of your family, and actually, I know you're not like them. But as long as their blood runs through your veins, they will hunt for you. They know no other way. Killing them would be the only way to stop them at this point, and doing so will make you a rogue. You would be no better than them," Haley says as she looks at me. It still amazes me how many shades of blue her eyes can change into, and it distracts me from my thoughts for a moment before reality seeps back in.

I wiggle uncomfortably, pushing myself onto the bed more. I've never thought about killing anyone, nor have I had a reason to kill anyone, but these assholes were making me have those thoughts. Why would I even want to talk to them anyway? They killed my parents. I should want to kill them, and hearing the words Haley just spoke makes my blood boil with anger.

"You're right Haley, why would I even think that talking to them was a good idea?" I say. God, I want to touch her so badly. I would kick her brother out and fuck her right here on his bed.

Yes, I know that doesn't sound right at all, but if you had the feelings of lust for her like I do, you would do the same. The vampire taking me over makes it even harder for me to restrain myself. My senses have hyped two hundred percent. She smells amazing—if amazing was a smell, that would be what she smells like.

"Earth to Austin!" Jonah says, clapping his hands in front of me. "You were so zoned out; you didn't hear anything I just said."

I shake my head and look around, realizing Haley had left the room. I guess I zoned out longer than I thought I did. "Where did she go?" I ask him.

"Your grandmother is back and my parents just got home. She's in the living room with them. The brothers were gone by the time they got here."

I push myself up off the bed and make my way into the room where everyone else was standing. Haley's parents, my grandmother, the Elders, and Haley were there. They looked as if they were having some kind of ritual. Athena is chanting words I don't understand, and the Elders were backing her with more words that make no sense to me.

I stand and watch as they all pass around a silver goblet and drink from it.

Once they've all taken their turns and it seems that whatever they were doing has finished, Haley walks over to me with a smirk on her face.

"What was that all about?" I ask.

"Athena and the Elders have magical powers. They were doing a ritual to protect us from those assholes," she replies, leaving it at that.

Jareth walks over to me and places his hand on my back. "Austin. Drake, Angelus, and myself are going to find the brothers and deal with them once and for all. I advise you not to leave this lair until you've heard back from us. Understood?"

I'm still dazed out a bit, but I understand what's going and agree to stay put until they come back with news.

Celina walks up to stand between Haley and I. "Your father and I have something to show you two once this Thompson problem has been taken care of. I promise this will all be over soon and you two will no longer be in danger. Austin, you are destined for great things." She just leaves it at that as she turns and walks away.

Well, that definitely got my mind racing. What great things? What do they have to show us?

I try to turn my thoughts to something normal because there is too much to speculate on at the moment.

Clothes.

I need more clothes. Yeah, I know that has nothing to do with what's going on at the moment, but it's an issue. I wonder if I'm still able to be in the daylight, or will I only be able to go out at night? I watch as Haley walks over to talk to her dad, and then I make my way over to my grandmother.

"Athena?"

"No Austin, you shouldn't call me by my first name. It's Grandmother to you, son."

I nod in agreement, knowing arguing with her on the point would do me no good. I frown as I notice everything looks a little different—either the light in here is getting better or my sight is just fucking with me.

"Did it just become brighter in here to you?" I ask her.

Laughing, she replies, "No that's just your sight being enhanced. You'll be able to see even on the darkest of nights, with no light at all. It's part of your gifts as a vampire."

"Well, I'm sure that will come in handy when walking the streets at night." I laugh.

She shakes her head and starts to walk away before I stop her.

"I wanted to talk to you more about the daywalker thing, if you don't mind. How will I know if I can go into the sun or not? Once I've sealed my bond with Haley, of course." I smirk.

"You shouldn't even think about going anywhere near the light of day until after you've mated. You need to be one hundred percent and have all of your strength. Then and only then, you can go somewhere the light shines from a crack above. You must only place no more than a hand into the light. If it burns you, you'll heal, but you'll know that you can no longer walk about the streets in the day time hours. All of these things will come to you. I know it's very confusing for you to take this all in at once, Austin. Just be patient and learn as you go. Like I said before, I'll be here for you and Haley when you need me," she finishes, excusing herself.

The Elders and Mr. Devile have already left, and Grandmother is saying her goodbyes. I find myself standing beside Haley.

"Haley, we need to contact Rob and Stacy to let them know what's going on. I'm sure they're wondering what the hell happened to us," I tell her as we walk away from the door where her mom and Athena are standing.

Chapter 22

HALEY

The smell of Austin walking up behind me is almost overwhelming. It smells like blood, chocolate, and lust. My skin tingles with excitement, but it's short lived when nothing sexy comes from his mouth.

He tells me we need contact Rob and Stacy as we move to stand behind the bar, and I agree with him.

"You've fed. Remember, I'm still human—well, kind of, but still, I need real food. I don't see myself living off of blood and raw meat anytime soon. It seems that my brother has nothing here to eat other than mac and cheese and some ramen noodles. So, we have to go into the city. It'll be dark soon, and safe for you to be out and about. The spell should keep the brothers away from us until the Elders can find them," I tell him.

It's so hard for me to keep my hands off of this man. His shirt is slightly ripped from when he fell earlier, his abs peeping through just enough to tease me, and it make heat rise between my legs. This isn't normal for me, maybe it's my vampire side lusting for this fine ass vampire man before me. Whatever it is, I'm liking it and can't wait to get my hands and mouth all over that body.

"Damn Haley, close your mouth, you're drooling," Austin says with a laugh.

"Fuck you Austin, I'm not drooling. Staring and daydreaming maybe, but drooling, I doubt very seriously. I'll

save that for when I'm licking those fine ass abs of yours."
Holy shit! Did I really just say that out loud?

"Ha-ha, really now," he replies.

"Shit, I can't believe I just said that to you Austin, I sounded so slutty."

"Oh, we'll both be slutty when I get to have you as my mate. Don't you worry, I'll have my mouth all over you, too. I can't wait to taste you."

"Damn Austin, you make me sound like your next meal." I reply with a giggle.

"Trust me Haley, you'll be more than just my meal," he says with an evil grin.

"I think we should end this while we can. Let's go tell mom what's going on and head out to contact Rob and Stacy."

I can tell he was getting a little happy in his manhood, and damn it looks huge, poking out of his pants while he tries to hide it behind the bar. I play it off like I'm not looking, but you know as well as I do, I was damn sure looking. *Whew, breathe. Just breathe.* I have my work cut out for me, being his mate—but I'm sure, from the looks of it, it's going to be a long, hard ride.

"Okay, just give me a minute to gather myself and I'll be ready to go. Why don't you go ahead and let Celina know what's going on, maybe have her contact your dad so he knows we're out in the city. Just in case we have any trouble with the douchebags," Austin informs me.

I remind him that I still need to eat, I've had nothing all day. "Maybe we can meet them for dinner someplace. I'm sure at this point in your change, human food isn't going to be something you want, though, so we can just grab me something on the fly. It's up to you," I say.

Once he's calmed his pants, we tell Mom and Jonah we're leaving and to make sure the locks are sealed behind us. Dad had given me a key while I was talking to him earlier.

The moment we step foot out the door and into the passageway, the sounds of feeding begin—I mean, it is what vampires do at night. Well, sex may not always be a part of it, but it's damn sure the loudest part of it. By the sounds of it, you would think these women have never had sex a day in their lives. Although, I'm sure fangs sinking into my neck would make me scream, too. Which makes me wonder what it's going to be like when Austin bites me during our mating. Will it be painful, or painfully erotic?

I'm having a lot of thoughts about this mating thing tonight, so I must be overly horny. But if you were me in the moment, as Austin looked into my eyes this morning and could have felt the wave of energy that filled my body... And let's not forget those damn abs, eyes, and all that was in his pants a while ago. It's enough to drive any woman crazy. Can you really blame me?

"We should be coming up on a door soon that will take us back into the city. I must warn that once we open the door at the end of the hallway, we'll be in a lounge, and it's in the back of an adult book store. It's the quickest way from my parents' place to get back into the city," I tell him.

I never remembered it being an adult book store growing up. But now that I think of it, my mom always covered my eyes until we were in the hallway. Maybe that's why I only remembered when she said, "Where the triangle meets the road, then there we must go." She was trying to distract me from seeing all those things.

"You must think I've never been in an adult store before, or maybe I've never watched porn." He starts laughing.

"Oh my God, Austin, you've watched porn?" I joke, covering my mouth with my right hand to try to hold back my laughter.

"Me? Never, I would do no such thing. I would rather be making my own porn with you," he says. Damn his voice gets deeper every time he speaks.

"The door should be just past this bar up here on the left. The other day when we came out of the door, there were people fucking against the wall outside the bar. Is this all still weird to you? It is just a normal day here in the underground world." Knowing it has to be weird, I still had to ask.

"It is for sure a lot to take in, and speaking of watching porn. It is like you're living in a porno down here. I am sure the more you're around, it the more accustomed you become to it. Will I have to live down here now, Haley? I mean, will we? Once you are my mate," He said, stopping to run his hand through his hair.

"We haven't gotten to that point yet, Austin. I don't quite know how to answer you on that one." What I really wanted to say was I would live in a cardboard box as long as he lived in it with me. Why am I so head over heels for this guy? Again, just a few days ago, he was a smart ass who didn't want to hear anything I had to say. Now he has me all googly eyed and acting like I'm in heat or some shit. Oh, let me add that once he did finally listen to me—well, he hasn't been able to keep his eyes off me since then.

"I guess we'll just figure it out together, huh?" He smiles and winks at me.

"There's the door, and yes we will," I tell him as he opens

the door, letting me enter first, then closing it behind him. The hallway into the store looks darker now than it did when I was here before. Maybe a light had blown.

I stop to let Austin catch up.

"Something doesn't feel right," I tell him as he moves closer. "I just have this feeling."

"Are there any voices, I mean people from the other side, speaking to you?"

I assure him that's not the case.

We continue on to the end of the hallway, coming upon the door that opens into the store. Once again, I can hear Tainted Love playing loudly on the speakers. Everywhere I've been with music, the song has played without fail. Maybe the shop plays it on a loop.

"Well, at least there are signs that your parents are still with us," I said, laughing as I let him again open the door for me. But this time, I hold it and insist that he go in before me. He pulls the lever on the wall, letting the door swing open.

"I agree. I guess it will now be our song, huh?" He laughs and walks into the room ahead of me.

I knew something wasn't right, and the person on the other side of the door just confirmed it. Hunter Thompson, the cousin of the trio of assholes. How did I not think about this one? I should have remembered he was always with them growing up, and did anything he could to just hang out with them.

He was pretty much their little bitch growing up. Standing with a smartass grin on his face, he's at least six feet tall, with brown bushy hair, a full beard, and tattoos on his biceps. He's much more muscular than his any of his asshole cousins, and his brown eyes have a look of despair in them. He could kick his cousins' asses with no problems, but once you're bonded to a vampire, you pretty much have to do as they say—and if you refused or tried to go against them, it could lead to your death. Unlike his cousins, he isn't a vampire. That's how they always had him in their control. Always promising him they would change him, because he wasn't born a vampire, not even a dhampir.

The way he has his arms crossed made me think he was waiting for a fight, but thankfully that wasn't the case when I ask him why he's there and what he wants. "I've been bonded to my cousins my whole life. I'm tired of it, and I don't want to be under their control any longer. I'll help you guys find them, if you help me find someone who can break my bond to them."

"How do we know you're not leading us into a trap? I don't really trust anyone with Thompson as their last name. Besides, how did you know we were coming this way?" I ask as the door closes behind us.

"I knew that you two would have to come back at some point when Brock told me he'd chased you guys away from your apartment. And remember the girl you threatened the other day when you came through here? Well, she's my sister." He grins.

"What? I do not remember you having a sister," I said, feeling surprise wash over me.

"I'm sure you don't remember a lot of things Haley, plus, you've never seen her with us. When we all hung out together, she lived with her dad in Mississippi. She came to live with us after he passed away a few years ago. The times she did come to visit, Mom wouldn't let her hang out with us. I mean, would you let your daughter hang out with a bunch of bloodthirsty vampires?"

Now that I think of it, I never went to his house. We

were always at my place or at Brocks, Brandon, and Bristol's place. But still, I don't remember him ever saying anything about a sister growing up, and he's right. If I were human, no way would I let my child hang out with these assholes.

"How did you know we would come back this way?" Austin chimes in.

"Well, actually, I didn't know for sure, but I figured if I came here enough that eventually you'd use this pathway again. After I got word that your vampire was taking control, I knew it would have to be at night. Seems I was spot on. Here we stand in the strip club worthy lounge in the back room of an adult sex shop." He smirks. Seems he was a smartass, just like his cousins.

"We have someplace to be so just give us your number... um, what's your name, anyway? We'll call you later," Austin tells him.

"Why don't you ask your girlfriend, she knows my name."

I chime in because I know this isn't going to end well otherwise, stepping between them. "His name is Hunter. Now Hunter, if you'll just give us a way to contact you and let us go, I promise we'll call you after we've taken care of everything we need to do in the city," I tell him as I move to push my way around him.

I can feel darkness in his soul when my arm brushes against him. I can also feel his sorrow, and the pain that he feels being bonded to his cousins. He grabs me by the arm, his grip is a little tighter then I would like it to be, but I can't let Austin see that it's hurting me. I'm still not sure how he'll react or how much strength he has at this point in his change. Hunter's not evil, I can tell by looking into his eyes.

All I can see is hurt, and how much he wants to be rid of the pain.

"I'll tell you now where they're hiding if you promise you'll call me, Haley. I can't be bonded to those assholes anymore. If they're killed, it will kill a part of me unless the bond is broken," he says.

I tell him about my friend the witch over at the bookstore, and tell him to let her know I sent him there. She can help him break his bond. I know Austin's grandmother could help, but I don't want to bring all of that upon his family.

Austin comes up, taking Hunter by the wrist to remove his hand from my arm. "Let her go, she's told you where to go for help. Now tell us where your asshole cousins are, so we can end all of this before anyone else gets hurt. You can give us your number, like I said before, and we'll contact you later to be sure everything goes well."

Finally, Hunter let go and we walked to the front of the store where his sister Jess was standing behind the counter, still looking like a teenage school girl in her uniform and pigtails. He asks her for a pen and paper so he can give us his number.

"Doing it the old school way, brother? Why don't you just save his number in your phone, like everyone else does these days?" Jess asks, trying to crack jokes.

I act as if I didn't hear anything she said and took the number from her brother. "Thank you, Hunter, now where can I tell my father and the Elders to find them?"

"They're staying in a warehouse on Lake street by the train tracks."

He gives us the address and we leave, promising we'll be in touch with him later. Once we are out of the store and onto the street, the familiar smell of burnt grease fills the cold night air. As weird as it may be, it makes me even more hungry. I should have worn a jacket, but at least I put on long sleeves over my tank top. We find a bench nearby, where we sit to call my father first to let him know the address we were given.

"We'll head there now, and I'll let you and Austin know if we find them," he says, hanging up faster than he answered. I'm sure I have a look of *what the hell just happened* on my face.

"What was that all about? You weren't on the phone for even a minute."

"I guess he was in a hurry to find the assholes. I didn't even have a chance to talk to him about Hunter telling me where they were," I reply.

Again, I had to make sure I don't touch him. This shit's getting really old. It's hard to keep myself from touching him. Our legs are only inches apart and I can feel the energy from him. I forgot that it was freezing cold outside the moment I sat down beside him.

"Maybe, you know how parents are," he replies.

Yeah well, he has no idea how my dad really is when he's in full hunter mode. He has one thing on his mind and that's taking out his prey. Yes, I said prey. It's just the same as hunting anything else in the world you all live in. Okay, maybe that sounds a little harsh, but at least the Elder brothers are with him, since it's up to them what their judgment will be. I reach into my pocket to pull out my phone again.

"I'm going to call Stacy to see if she can pick us up and take us to my place to grab our things. I think I'll just grab food while I'm at home also. The smell of the burnt grease made me hungrier at first, but now it's making my stomach churn. I'm sure you're not loving the smell either," I say to him.

"It smells a-fucking-mazing." He laughs. "Yeah, I'm good with that, hopefully she isn't busy and can help us out. Maybe she'll have some news from Rob, about my car. Will I even need a car anymore? Maybe I should just talk to him about selling it," Austin says as he stands up from the bench to pace from one side of the walkway to the other.

"Stacy said she's on her way. I'm so glad I have a friend like her. I don't know what I would do without her," I say.

Austin stops walking "That reminds me. She said she was sent to the store to keep an eye on me. I wonder who the person was that sent her to do so?"

Chapter 23
AUSTIN

I can no longer feel the cold of the night—it feels the same to me as it did before we came outside. Haley, however, claims she's freezing. Maybe it's my nerves or adrenaline from the whole vampire thing. So many questions, so many things to learn. Stacy pulls up while I'm in deep thought, and we get into her SUV before I notice Rob was driving and not Stacy. I knew those two were a thing the whole time they were trying to play it off. I wait until we start moving and after we've thanked them for picking us up, before I have to ask.

"Stacy, I've been thinking since the other day when you told me you were sent to work at the store to keep an eye on me. Can you tell me who sent you, and how did they know you would get a job at the market?"

"I was sworn never to tell you, but from what Haley's told me, I'm sure you've already met your grandmother. She sent me when she felt that you were in some kind of danger. Her and Mr. Jones have been friends for years, but she threatened his life if he told you she was alive. She's also the reason you got the job there. She knew you were in a safe place and the Jones' have been keeping watch over the Shreveport coven for many, many years."

"Your grandmother tried to keep you away from the coven in hopes you would stay protected. It wasn't until she knew the Thompsons were after you, and she found out you and Haley were fated mates. She knew you two were fated before anyone else. Once all of this came to be, she realized she had no choice but to bring you into the coven. I was just talking to her earlier today before she flashed without warning and left me standing on the street. I have no idea where she had to be in such a hurry," Stacy replies.

"We have a good idea where she had to be. I'm sure she told you that Austin is changing and his vampire is taking over. Well, he's at the point when he needs to feed on blood. I had to call her to come help, because I couldn't get my parents to respond to phone calls or to me telepathically. I didn't know it was blood he needed. I thought he was going to die, so I freaked out," Haley tells her, turning to look over at me with a slight grin on her face and a blush in her cheeks.

I smile back and kind of just slide down in the seat, not responding to what Stacy just said. I still wish my grandmother hadn't stayed hidden for so many years, even if she did it to keep me safe. I feel like I've missed out on so much in my life by not knowing her, or the vampire and coven side of my family. All the shit my parents kept hidden from me just to keep me safe, and they still had to die—only for me to be chased by some rogue ass vampires and become a bloodsucker myself.

I have to push all of that behind me, and let the past be just that, the past. As hard as it may be, it's something that has to be done. I have a new life now.

My new life is with Haley. I'm not sure where that's going either, but one thing I do know is I never want to spend another day without her by my side. I never thought the girl I spent the rest of my life with would become my "mate" within just a few days of meeting her. It's not a bad thing, since we're fated. The world knew we were meant to be mates. Fate brought us together, even though I wanted to run that first day. Now I only want to run *to* her. Not *away* from her.

Okay, that's enough of my mushy ass thoughts for now.

"Stacy, I thought the two of you were just friends. Seems like you and Rob have been spending a lot of time together," I say jokingly.

"I don't remember ever saying *just friends,* Austin, I think I may have just said my friend Rob. We've been talking for a while now. We've just never officially said boyfriend or girlfriend yet. Right, Rob?" she says while putting her hand on his thigh.

"Well, who the hell needs labels, anyway?" He replies while laughing under his breath.

Stacy laughs, knowing he was only joking, and Haley and I join in, as well.

"Well, I guess the two of you have a label, huh? Seeing that you're now mates, according to the Elders." Rob looks at me and the laughing stops.

I just give him a blank stare for a few seconds before I start laughing again. "Hmm, mates, Haley. How do you feel about being the fated mate to a guy from the streets who's destined to become a vampire?" I look at her and grin.

"It's all still a little weird, but I think I could get used to it. Besides, I'm half vampire myself. What about those two up there, dhampir and werewolf. Does that mean if you two ever have kids, they'll be hybrids?" Haley says with a stunned look on her face.

"It means it will be a bad ass mofo," Rob turns to tell her.

We finally make it to Haley's apartment complex, after what seemed like hours riding in the backseat of this car. I walked up the stairs that I ran up the last time we were here. If my strength is supposed to be enhanced, why do I feel so tired, just from climbing up a few flights of stairs? I have to stop and sit on the bottom step of the last flight.

"I'm not sure what's going on, guys. I feel like I've used all of my energy."

Haley turned around and came back down to where I'm sitting on the hunter green steps. They feel like a block of ice under my ass. Now that I think about it, *I* feel like a block of ice. My body's freezing now. An hour ago, I couldn't tell it was even cold out.

"Athena said you should have had enough blood to get you through a few days."

"Athena, as in his grandmother?" Rob asks.

"Yes, my grandmother, why do you ask?" I reply.

"Because her blood is your family's blood. Which means the blood you drink from her is the pretty much the same blood already inside your body. You burned through it faster than you would any other blood. You need to feed again," he tells me.

"How did she not know that? She of all people should have known," I say in a panic.

This vampire shit is a lot more painful and drawn out than I ever imagined it would be. I guess my change is different than one who has been bitten by a bloodsucker. Not that I know how any of this shit works, but if I need to feed to get my energy back up, then so be it.

"Just what or whom am I supposed to feed on, Rob? I can't take blood from Haley, and Stacy doesn't look like she's willing to offer up her wrists, seeing how she's walking backwards up the stairs."

"You can take my blood," he says as his fangs pops out to

bite his wrist. "Go ahead, I'm man enough to handle it. Besides, I'm a shifter and it'll heal within minutes. We claim our mates by biting each other, so you drinking my blood is no big deal. I will warn you, though. Whoever you feed from, you'll always have some kind of connection with them. Once you feed from my arm, it may or may not create a bond between us."

He's full of information, but all I am worried about in that moment is the blood pouring from his wrist. The smell of copper and wet dog fills the air. He bends down to place his arm in front of me. I can't control myself once the smell of blood is stronger, and I grab his wrist and begin to suck. The warm blood coats my throat and I can feel the power of his wolf running through me. I feel my strength building back, and the energy pouring from him is almost over-whelming. I see flashes of his werewolf running through my head, and suddenly he says, "Enough."

"You were enjoying that a little more than you should have. You were playing inside my head. Austin, you have powers beyond anything you can imagine. I could feel you in my thoughts," he says while I'm still holding his arm to my mouth.

Shit just keeps getting weirder.

"I have no idea how or why it happened. After I started drinking from you, I could see you changing into your wolf. You were running to someone, but you stopped me before I could see who the person was," I reply.

"It was my mom. I could see you there, Austin. They took my mom away from the pack when I was younger. I haven't seen her since. I was running to try to stop them. I ended up running away from our pack soon after and came to Louisiana.

Looks like we did bond. You're stuck with me for the rest of your life now, whether you like it or not. Even if we're miles away, we'll still be able to read each other's thoughts." Rob looks down at me before taking his arm from my hands.

"How come you never told me this, Rob?" Stacy asks with a look of disbelief on her face.

"It never came up in conversation, and I've always enjoyed our time together. I didn't want to ruin it with sob stories of my old pack," he tells her while wrapping his arm over her shoulder. "We'll talk about it later, okay. I love you, Stacy."

She blushes, laying her head on his chest with a smile. "You've never said that Rob, not even after I told you I love you."

"First time for everything." Rob grins and turns to walk up the stairs with her still on his arm.

"Now, let's focus on why we're here. We have to get their things and get Austin back before his change is complete, and from the looks of it that won't be long. Maybe just hours even," he tells us.

It seemed for a moment those two had forgotten that Haley and I were even here. I stand, pushing myself and holding onto the rail. Haley reaches to help me, but pulls away once she remembers yet again that we should not touch until my change is complete—and that can't happen soon enough.

Climbing the last flight of stairs is a breeze. Haley walks over and unlocks the door, letting us all go in first, and she follows behind, making sure to lock the door as soon as it closes. She walks into the small kitchen and opens the freezer.

"I have a couple of pizzas in here if you guys are hungry."

"Pizza. That sounds so good, but can I still eat pizza? I mean, I just had werewolf blood and I'm pretty full," I joke.

"I don't know if you can or not, but I sure as hell can. I've also had this tasty were blood you speak of. What? Why are you two looking at me like that? I'm part vampire too, you know. My fangs work just the same." Stacy laughs.

"Wait, you have fangs, too? I thought I was the only dhampir with fangs," Haley says while taking the pizzas out of the freezer, placing them on the pan, and then into the oven.

"I sure do, and I love the taste of blood during sex. It's my weakness. I'm sure you'll feel the same once you and Austin get to mate, fuck, screw. Whatever it is that you two will do once he turns full vampire." Stacy smirks, throws her hair over her shoulder, and walks over to sit beside Rob on the couch.

The thought of Haley drinking my blood sends a shockwave straight to my cock. Then the thought of her sucking my cock after drinking my blood quickly followed. Fuck, I have to stop thinking this shit in front of Rob and Stacy. I'm sure these pants I'm wearing won't cover my massive hard on. As a matter of fact, I already know they don't hide anything after seeing the look on Haley's face back at the lair.

I turn my back to them, facing toward where Haley's standing in the kitchen, and she looks at my eyes first and then my crotch. She blushes, and then a grin spreads across her face.

"I need to grab my clothes out of your dryer," I say to her

as she comes as close as she can without touching and whispers in my ear.

"I think that may be a good idea, and I can't wait to take care of that problem you keep having when the time comes."

Damn it, Haley. I just want to grab her by her neck, kiss her, taste her, and take her right here on the kitchen counter. I wouldn't even give a shit if anyone else was in the room at this point. But I think it's best I just get my clothes from her dryer and let my cock ache with need. This change has sent my sexual desires into maximum overdrive. My senses are hyped more than I could even express to anyone who hasn't been through this. Maybe once the change is complete, I'll have better control of it all.

Chapter 24

HALEY

Austin can't seem to control his manhood lately. Not that I want him to control it—hell, I want to order him to release his pent-up sexual frustration. On me.

Okay, stop with the dirty thoughts, Haley. Pizza, yes, check the pizza.

"Hey guys, the pizzas are done if you're hungry," I say while placing them on the small, round, wooden table I have in my dining space before sitting a stack of paper plates and napkins down beside them.

"I hate to rush everyone, but Austin and I need to be back as soon as possible. I have no idea when he'll have another episode or when he'll complete his change. I just think it may be best if we are back underground before he does so," I say, placing my plate of pizza on the bar.

Austin returns from my bedroom with his clothes in one of my gym bags. Sadly, he doesn't have any more than that. I wish I could say the same. I have two-bedroom closets full of clothes. I have to make a choice of what to take with me back to my parents' place.

He tries to eat the pizza, but it doesn't go over very well.

"Well, pizza still taste amazing, probably even more amazing than before. But once it hits my stomach, I feel like I'm going to throw it back up," Austin tells me.

"You'll be fine, your body is just rejecting food. You'll soon only be able to eat raw meat, or blood," I reply while I put the rest of the pizza in a couple of Ziplock bags. I'll take it back for my brother, lord knows that kid can put away some food.

"Let me grabs some things and we'll get going, if you guys are ready to head back, Stacy?" I ask them while I'm walking into my bedroom, not really giving them time to reply.

I know Austin will complete his change soon, and I have no idea how it'll affect him. The city is not the best place for us to be when it happens, just in case he freaks out or goes on a rampage. I really don't see that happening with him, but when humans turn, they all react in different ways. Just because I think it wouldn't happen doesn't mean it can't.

Either way, it's best to be safe in our part of the city, instead of being out where humans could see him change or possibly become his next meal. He'll need to feed again once it's complete. I'm hoping I'll be the one he feeds on next. The thought of him digging his fangs into my neck while his cock is deep inside me makes me blush. I walk back into the kitchen after grabbing my things from my room and picked up the pizza I had bagged for Jonah, stuffing it into the bag with my clothes.

"I'm ready when you guys are. We need to get Austin back underground before his change is complete."

I walk toward the door, again without giving them a chance to respond. Maybe I'm being a little pushy or even an asshole. But if this happens out here, it could be much worse than me being a little bit of an asshole towards my friends. I'm sure they understand, as they've both seen the change from human to vampire, as well to shifter. So, they both know as well as I do that we can't predict what is to come of his change.

This is my first time seeing a dhampir change without first dying. I guess it's like I was thinking before—Austin is dying and the vampire is living. He'll still have the mind and body he's always had, but he'll now be thinking and acting as a vampire. The dark side of him will come forward, even if it's not evil. We all have a dark side—some of us just keep it hidden better than others.

"I hope you have a jacket Haley. You're in such a hurry to leave, but you know it's cold out there," Austin informs me while almost placing his hand on my back. The heat can be felt even with him being inches away from touching me.

I turn to look over my shoulder at him. "I knew I was forgetting something. I just want to make sure you're in a safe place when the time comes. I guess I have too much on my mind," I tell him, grabbing my jacket from the coat closet next to the front door. I also grab a hoodie for him to use, as I know that long sleeve plaid shirt he has on isn't enough to keep him warm.

Does he even feel the cold anymore? I know my parent have always told us that temperature changes didn't really affect them unless it was extreme heat, much hotter than our summers in Louisiana. And they're already pretty extreme if you ask me or any other human that has to live with the humid heat in midsummer.

"As soon as we're on the road, I need to call Hunter." I look over at Austin, noticing he doesn't look very pleased with the idea.

"Can we really trust him, Haley?"

The worried look eases from his face once I look him in the eyes. "He did give us a lead to find where his cousins were hiding out." I grin with a shrug.

"He did indeed, but he also asked for something in

return, am I right? We'll just have to keep a close eye on that guy. Something still doesn't sit right with me," Austin tells me as he turns to look out the window at passing traffic.

I let him have his moment to think for a bit while I call my dad. The phone never rings more than three times before he picks up, even with the shit service we have under the city. This time it rings at least six before he finally answers.

"Haley, I have to call you back!" he says as he hangs up the phone.

Him hanging up on me is really getting old. I nudge Austin with my phone to get his attention.

"They have to be having some problems, Austin. He sounded winded and said he would call me back. Vampires don't get winded that easy," I tell him.

"I'm sure they're fine. They're much more powerful than the Thompsons. I don't think your dad and the Elders would have any problems there," he assures me.

"I guess you're right," I reply, picking up my phone again to call Hunter.

"Hello?" he answers rather quickly.

"Hey Hunter, this is Haley. I was just calling to see how things went with Mrs. Hyde, and to ask if you've had any trouble from your cousins?"

"Hi Haley. She did a spell to break the bond, but she said that I must be bonded to someone else before the blood moon or the spell would be broken. The bond from someone else would forever break my bond with those fuckers."

"Can you meet us back at the shop where your sister works? We'll get you answers from Athena, Austin's grand-mother. Oh, and have you heard from those fuckers?"

"Trust me, I know who Athena is, and I'm not sure bringing me to her will go over very well if she thinks I had anything to do with her son's murder. As far as my cousins go, I haven't heard a peep from them since I told you where they were. I'm hoping that means they've been taken care of. And yes, I'll meet you back at the shop. See you then," he finishes, hanging up the phone.

The look Austin's giving me when I turn to look at him kind of sends a shock through me, but not a good one this time.

"Why would you take that asshole to my grandmother for help?" he groans.

"Do you not see that he helped you, Austin? Had he not told us where to find those guys, they wouldn't have stopped until you were dead," I say, thinking to myself that the darkness must be fighting to take over the light in Austin. He seems so angry in the moment.

"Sorry, Haley. I'm not sure what's come over me. It was as if all I could think after I heard you talking to him were evil thoughts. Maybe it's me trying to protect my mate and my family. You're right, once again. I know he helped and it's only right that we help him break the bond." A smile comes back to brighten his face.

I nod. "It's okay Austin, you've had a lot to deal with today. You have to learn to control the evil thoughts. The darkness will overcome you if you don't fight it off. Once you change, this will become harder for you to do, but you must. Giving into the darkness will forever tie you to evil."

Chapter 25
AUSTIN

I'm not sure what came over me, knowing she was on the phone with that man, offering him help from my grandmother. All I could think was I wanted to kill him and those fuckers he's bonded to for what they'd done to my parents. But there's a part of me that also knows if he had anything to do with it, it was to only save his own life from his shitty family. I'm sure he feared they would kill him, as well.

I don't like having this evilness overcome me like this. I have always been a kind-hearted guy, and even knowing what they had done to my parents before my change started, the thought of killing them never crossed my mind. Once Haley explains that it's the darkness trying to overcome me, I totally understand. And I have an instant calmness wash over me as she smiles and I see the glint in her eyes. She's the most beautiful being on the planet. Hell, the universe, for that matter. How the hell did a guy like me get so damn lucky to have her as his fated mate? The only catch is that the old me has to die for my vampire to have his mate.

"Sorry, Haley. I'm not sure what's come over me. It was as if all I could think after I heard you talking to him were evil thoughts. Maybe it's me trying to protect my mate and my family. You're right, once again. I know he helped and it's only right that we help him break the bond." I smile back at her. "What did you mean by saying my grandmother can help him though?" The smile leaves my face as I wait for her to answer.

"He said Mrs. Hyde had done a spell to break his bond from the cousins, but if he hadn't bonded to someone else before the next blood moon, the spell would not work and his bond with them would be unbreakable. Athena was the first person that I thought of and if anyone would have answers, it would be her. We could have gone to the Elders, but they have to deal with the problems of the whole Shreveport coven, and I don't want to keep them busy with our problems all the time. Besides, your grandmother may as well be one of the Elders. She has as much, if not more, wisdom than any of them do." Haley pauses to catch her breath.

"I'm also sorry I didn't ask you first before assuming you'd be okay with her helping him. I can understand why you'd be upset. I really do think he's a good guy, Austin. I could feel the pain inside of him when he bumped into me earlier," she tells me.

We've completely forgotten that anyone else was in the car with us while we were having our conversation, but I don't think they paid us any mind. Seeing them hold hands made it hard for me to not reach over and grab Haley's. Damn this change can't be complete soon enough. The moment I'm finally able to hold her, I may never let her go.

"Okay guys, we're here," I hear Stacy say from the front seat.

Damn, that was a quick trip back. I really must have been lost in thought the whole way.

"Thank you, Stacy and Rob, you guys have no idea how big a help you've been to us. I hope that one day, I'll be able to repay the two of you," I tell them while helping Haley grab her bags.

"It's what friends do, Austin. And those of us from the Other World have to stick together and help each other. We have too much evil already. Besides, we're bonded now. We have no other choice but to be there for each other," Rob replies while stepping out of the car to shake my hand. "You're part of my pack now, whether you like it or not."

Stacy's standing beside him and I move to hug her.

"Thank you for everything. You've got a good wolfman there, Stacy." I laugh.

"Ha, ha, ha, thank you Austin, he's all right I suppose. And anytime," she replies while getting back into the car.

The digital thermometer on the bank across the street says it's thirty-one degrees. It's still not cold to me, but I know it has to be for Haley.

"Let's get you inside, you must be freezing. I can no longer tell the difference in temperature change." I take her bags and motion her toward the door.

Once inside the shop, we ask the lady at the counter if Jess was working, but she'd already left for the day. "Her brother just came in though, and he went to the back. Are you the ones he was supposed to be meeting here? Are you two vampires?" she asks us while still standing behind the counter.

I don't think I'm ready to admit that I'm a vampire just yet. I mean, I do still have a little of my human side —for now.

"We would be the ones he's waiting for, yes. I'm not sure what you mean by vampire. There's no such thing." I smile as innocently as I can at the lady.

"Don't play dumb with me dude, I know about the secret

passages and tunnels below the city. I work here, remember? We see them come and go all the time," she says as she walks around the counter, reaching out to shake my hand. "I'm Brinley."

I took her hand but only for a second. She's not human, but it's not my place to call her out. It's a strong sent of woods, wet dog, and sunflower perfume. She has very striking features. Her dark brown hair falls to her shoulders, she has brown eyes, and a very defined jawline you don't find on most females. The shirt she's wearing looks like it may be a few sizes too small.

"Nice to meet you, Brinley," Haley says, putting herself between the two of us.

"Oh, you must be Haley. Hunter told me about you two and the trouble you've been having with his shithead cousins. I'm not trying to hit on your man. It's Hunter I'm after. I mean, have you seen those damn stocky arms of his?" Brinley swishes her hair and starts to walk away. "He's waiting for you guys in the back room. Good luck and be safe."

I look down at Haley and motion toward the back, forgetting everything the other lady just said. I pushed the curtain open, finding Hunter pacing the floor like he's waiting for someone to give birth.

"Thank God you guys are finally here!" he says, excitement in his voice.

I guess I would be just as excited too if I knew I was soon going to be free of the evil his cousins have bestowed upon him. I smile, still not sure I fully trust this guy, but I'll take it like I'm just I'm returning the favor.

"I only have a few days. I Googled to check and the next blood moon is only three days away. I hope your grandmother can help me figure this out, Austin. I can't thank you guys enough for this," he says as he calmly walks to the bookshelf and pulls the book forward to open the passageway door.

"Just remember, if we help you and you're just leading us into a trap, I will kill you. Do you understand, Hunter? I will not let anything happen to my mate or my family," I let him know, walking into the open doorway behind Haley.

Again, I feel evil building up inside me. The urge to mate overcomes me. I know it isn't long before my human side will be lost. I can tell my vampire is on edge, pushing to take over. Haley turns to look at me over her shoulder. She seems worried but before I could ask her what was wrong, I feel Hunter's hands on my back as I start to fall to the floor yet again. How many fucking times am I going to get weak like this before the vampire is strong enough to sustain me? My eyes close and I feel myself slip away again.

Chapter 26
HALEY

Damn it, Austin has become weak again and almost falls to the floor. Thankfully Hunter was here to catch him. Austin's body begins to shiver and his eyes roll back into his head. I know I'm not supposed to touch him until we're mated, but I couldn't help myself. I push my hand behind his neck to give him comfort. The moment my hand connects to the skin on his neck—a shock, like the hottest of fire, runs through my arm and into my body, and it hits me hard enough that if a body could have an orgasm from a single touch, it just happened to me.

Austin's fangs burst forth from his gums, and his eyes go back to normal. Well, by normal, I mean no longer rolling back into his head. They're an ice blue, cold with a red rim around his pupil. Stunning if you ask me, but others may find it frightening.

"Haley, what's going on here?" Hunter asks, and the look he gives me is nothing short of shocked by what had just happened.

"Austin is becoming a vampire. I think his change has just been completed. We need to get him to his grandmother as soon as possible. Let's get out of this passage and into the underground, and I'll summon for her. She can help us with your problems and let us know what to do from here with Austin. You have to help him, Hunter. I wasn't supposed to touch him until we were mated. I'm not sure why, but after what I just felt, I think it's best that I don't touch him again for now," I reply tell him as he reaches to put Austin's arm around his shoulder.

Once we're safe in our world, Hunter helps Austin down to sit against the dingy wall. I move away for a bit to call out to Athena.

"Austin had another spell. I think his change is complete. If you can you hear me, please come."

I hope I'm not too far from her that she can't hear my call. "Athena." I repeat myself a few times before I hear a faint voice. "I hear you Haley, tell me where you are."

Just like before, she's here before I could finish letting her know where we were. Damn, I hate that I'm not able to flash from place to place like that. Austin is sitting against the wall when she arrives. He looks like nothing has even happened. As a matter of fact, he looks even better than he did just moments before his episode.

"I'm fine. I don't know why she called you. It could have waited. I'm fine, I just got dizzy, that's all," he tells us.

I think he's lying, but I have to take his word that he's fine. Athena seems to have forgotten the reason I called her here anyway and has taken notice of the other guy standing next to me. A shiver runs down my back from the look that she's giving me. Austin stands from where he was sitting and comes to stand next to me.

"Why do we have a Thompson in our midst?" Athena asks, eyes narrowed.

"You must not have talked to the Elders. He helped us find his cousins. He's always been bonded to them. He's been to the witch at the bookstore, and she did a spell to break the bond, but it's only temporary. He must be bonded to another before the blood moon," I answer.

"It was not my choice, but he helped find the ones who are out to kill me. Besides, if he wanted to harm me, he's already had plenty of time and opportunity to do so," Austin chimes in.

"If you two trust him, then so be it." She smirks, walking over to look at Austin's neck. I hadn't noticed that on his neck was the perfect shape of my hand where I lifted his neck earlier.

"You touched him. I told you two not to touch until his change was complete."

"It was only for a brief moment to lift his neck. Once I felt the heat from him and the shock that ran through me, I let him go. I'm sorry, but I thought he was hurting and I lifted his neck to help him breathe," I reply.

"It's only a minor burn, and it will heal once he has mated and fed from you. I advise you not to do anymore touching before then. It won't be a good idea for anyone around you at that moment. His change is complete and his urge to mate will overcome him. He is to feed from you before the blood moon," the grandmother explains.

It's still a little odd that she talks to us about mating, but I just nod my head in agreement. It's also kind of embarrassing that Hunter's standing here, listening to her talking about the two of us, and I can't help my blush.

"Austin, are you sure you're okay?" I ask, changing the subject.

"I've never felt better."

The sound of his voice was muffled by the sudden sound of gunshots, and then another voice rings out.

"Athena, get them out of here!"

It was my dad's voice. I'd know that voice anywhere.

"Grab my arm, all of you! *Now*!" she yells loudly.

Before everything turned black, I heard another gunshot and a loud groan coming from Hunter.

"I've been shot," Hunter says as we are all suddenly standing in my parents' lair.

Athena must have flashed us all here. I had no idea I would even be able to withstand the flash without any harm, but at the moment, that's the least of my worries.

"Where are you hit, Hunter?" I ask him as he eases himself down to lay on the floor.

"I've been hit in my abdomen. It was them. My fucking cousin shot me."

His voice sounds weak and threadbare. I looked down, and the blood was more than I'd expected. I run to grab towels to put pressure on it, and I glance up at Austin. He has his fangs out, glaring down at me. The smell of blood has over taken his sense and he isn't hiding the fact.

"I am dying, don't let me die," Hunter moans, clutching at his wound.

"Austin, you must change him. It's the only way. He has lost too much blood. Become his sire," Athena tells him.

"What the hell is a sire, and how the hell do I change someone?" Austin replies, a look of frustration covering his face.

"A sire means you have control over him once you've changed him. He will forever be bonded to you and under your control. You must drink from him, and then feed him your blood. He will begin to heal and he will slowly change into one of us. It's the only way at this point—otherwise he dies, and his death will be on your hands," his grandmother tells him, leading him over to where Hunter is lying on the floor.

"Hold on, what do you mean I'll have control over him? I

don't want to be in control of someone, or even some*thing* for that matter. I just became a vampire less than an hour ago. I can't even control myself at this point."

"Please Austin, don't let me die. Change me," Hunter begs while more of his blood starts to puddle on the floor.

Chapter 27
AUSTIN

I lied when I said I was okay. I'm so dizzy, I can hardly stand. I felt the change take over my body. Everything turned black, and the darkness overcame me. As soon as I come to my senses, a gun shot rang out and we've been flashed to the Devile lair.

I was thinking humans couldn't flash like vampires could, but it seems Haley made the journey just fine. But then there's Hunter, telling us he'd been shot and it was his cousin who'd fired the shot that hit him in his abdomen. He's crying, begging us not to let him die while Haley is pressing towels on his wound, trying to stop the bleeding. I'm still in a daze and not clear on what's fully happened when my grandmother insists that I change him.

"Austin, you must change him. It's the only way. He's lost too much blood. Become his sire."

I have no fucking clue what a sire is, and even after she explains it to me, I still have no idea what it is that I am to do. She tells me that I will be in control of him and forever bonded—whatever that means. I don't even know if I can control myself at this point. It hasn't even been an hour since I became a vampire and now, I'm being told to change someone.

"Are you sure? Wouldn't it be best to let him die? He'll become a bloodsucking monster if he's like his cousins.

Besides, he's a Thompson! How do we know he won't turn on us once he has changed?" I ask.

"Like I said, if he dies his death is no longer on his cousin, it will forever be on you. Austin, change him now. Before it's too late. I wouldn't have asked you to do it had I thought he was a threat," Athena says, taking my hand and leading me over to where Hunter is lying on the floor.

The towels Haley have covering his wound are no longer stopping the blood, and it's now started to puddle on the floor around him. A look of shock covers his face, and his stare is blank. The copper smell of his blood fills my senses, it's so strong I can practically taste the metallic bitterness, and my need to taste it overwhelms me.

"Please, Austin. Don't let me die. Change me," Hunter begs, reaching his hand up toward me.

Within seconds, I've moved behind him. I lifted him from the floor, sinking my fangs deep into the crook of his neck. A gasp of air escapes him, then a high-pitched scream once I start to drink his blood. I feel his body going limp as his life source flows into my mouth. His life is slipping away beneath my fangs, and I don't want to stop until I have taken it all. Every drop of his blood, his life.

"Enough, Austin!" Athena brings me back to reality. "You must stop, he's close enough to death. He needs to drink your blood now, he must be turned," she continues.

Either way, I'll have to live with him for the rest of my vampire life—alive or dead. Dead I would be haunted with his death. Alive I am haunted by being his sire, and I still have no idea what that even means. I snatch my fangs from his neck, leaving the holes to bleed, watching as blood ran down his neck and onto his chest.

I hadn't noticed that his shirt had somehow been

removed completely until I followed the trail of blood. I hoped to leave my mark to remind him who gave him life again after losing it to his family. He will no longer be bonded to his cousins, but forever in my debt. I watched the blood flow from his neck down his chest, and right back to the wound where he had been shot, and for once in my life, I feel powerful.

I raise my wrist to my mouth and bite down, pushing my fangs into my vein. Releasing the blood, letting it pour from my arm, I reach down and place it against his lips, forcing him open his mouth.

"Take it Hunter, drink it or die! I don't give a shit either way," I tell him.

Haley moves behind me, easing the evil that has started to overtake me. I really don't want him to die—or do I? No, no. I don't, he must live and forever be in my debt. Forever one of us, no longer cursed by his evil past. But yet cursed as a bloodsucker, changed by a member of the enemy's family.

The family that his cousins thought they were taking out. Hunter's body begins to shake under my wrist, and his head falls upon my chest as his eyes roll back into his head. The color begins to leave his face, and he stops sucking on the blood pouring from my wrist.

"Keep it there, he must continue to take your blood," Haley says, and it makes me wonder just how many humans she's watched someone become a vampire.

I keep my wrist lying on his lips, letting my blood run down his throat, uncomfortably letting his body lie back against mine. I then noticed another person has come into the room.

"Hello Celina, how long have you been standing there?" I ask, not even knowing when she'd come into the room. I guess I have more pressing matters at hand—or wrist, as the case may be. I laugh to myself at my own corny joke.

"I've been here the whole time. Well I was in my chamber, and I came out once I heard the loud scream. Angelus already called to let me know what happened. I just didn't realize that you all had ended up here. He didn't know if anyone was hit by the gunfire, but he knew that you two were protected by the spell that was put in place by the Elders and Athena. Speaking of, Athena, now that you have talked Austin into changing this man and saving his life, what are we to do with him? We can't just send a newbie running the streets of Shreveport." Celina twists her hair as she waits for Athena to answer.

Hunter's eyes have closed and he begins to shiver as his head pushes back hard into my chest. I ease him down, letting him lie on the floor beside me, not wanting to keep him from shifting back and forth. It had to be uncomfortable, the way he was laying against me. Standing, I walk over next to my grandmother.

"I'll take care of him. We'll have a nice place for him to stay in the Elder's chambers for a while. I'm pretty sure I can talk them into it. I think," Athena says, lowering her head to look down at Hunter. The blood has started to dry from his wound—wait, no. The wound is gone. It was completely healed.

"What the hell is going on here?" I look at Celina and then Haley with what I was sure was a very confused look on my face. "How did the gunshot wound just close up and heal that fast? Did my blood do that to him?"

They giggle, while I just stand here staring at them, waiting for them to tell me how this happened.

"Do you not remember that vampires heal almost

instantly? Once you changed him, his wounds began to heal. You still have a lot to learn about your new vampire ways, Austin. You also may be the very first vampire to become a sire on your first day," Celina says as her cell phone rings from the kitchen counter.

"Hello, yes they're here and safe. Well, other than Hunter. He was shot and Austin had to turn him. Oh yeah, by the way, Austin's change is complete. You captured all three of them? That's great, but I hate that one of them had to lose a life. Okay honey, we'll see you when you get here." I overhear her replies back to the person on the other end of the phone, who I assume is Mr. Devile. I mean, who else would she be calling honey?

"Your father will be back here soon. They've captured all three brothers, but Brandon, the one who shot Hunter, lost his life. Brock and Bristol have been taken to lock down at the chambers. Once he gets here, I need to keep my promise. I have a secret to share with you and Austin." Celina walks toward Haley and puts her arm around her shoulder.

I could feel pain coming from Haley at the thought of one of her childhood friends losing his life, but I could also tell that she knew it was for the best. Because he wasn't aiming that gun at Hunter when those shots were fired. Once her mom's arm wraps around her and tells her she has a secret to share with us, a slight smile lights her face. I'm still weary of not touching her before mating, and I want nothing more than to walk over and wrap my arms around her for comfort.

For a moment, it seemed we'd all forgotten that Hunter was still laying on the floor—well, he had been, but now he was sitting up and beginning to look around. All the color was now gone from his skin, and his eyes were a brighter shade of brown, though sunk back more into his sockets. His muscles seem more defined than before.

"Everything is so bright, the colors so vivid. I can smell every person in the room by their own scent." Hunter looks up at me and then to Athena, looking as if he needs an explanation.

"You've only just begun to notice things child; it's been only minutes since you became one of us. I'll take you to the Elders, and they'll prepare a room for you in the chambers for a couple of days. No worries, you'll be far away from the cells your cousins now call home, as they are farther underground than we are. I promise you'll be safe and this is the best thing. You must learn to control your new powers, and you need to feed. You have to learn to control the darkness inside you, rather than let the darkness control you," Athena tells him, reaching down for him to take her by the hand.

"Will I have to stay down here forever? Can I return to the city above at all? What will we tell my family?" Hunter worries as he takes her hand and stands with her help.

"We'll take care of all of that in due time. For now, we need to find you a willing host to feed upon. Let's be on our way. We can catch up with Austin again soon." She speaks to him with a soft, soothing voice as they walk to the door.

Hunter turns and comes to stand in front of me, stopping within a few inches from my face.

"Is this what you think is best for me, sire? I mean, um… Austin?" he asks me.

Someone asking for my approval was a little odd. Looking him in the eyes with a stern gaze, I place my hand behind his neck.

"This is new to me as well, Hunter. We'll learn this all as we go. For now, I think it best you do as Athena says. I'll pay you a visit within a few days. You're in good hands, I can assure you that," I reply, moving my hand down to his back and turning him to walk toward the door.

Athena reaches out her hand, offering a smile. Once he places his hand into hers, they flash. Just like that they were gone, and Hunter had no choice but to go with her. I know it's best for him, and me as well, at the moment. Besides, I have to learn my own powers and what to do now that I'm a vampire.

I walk over to Haley, wondering how it is that we aren't mated yet, but I can still feel her energy.

Like it feeds my cold dark soul.

Do I still have a soul?

There were so many things I still needed to know.

Chapter 28

HALEY

Thankfully, me touching Austin as he completed his change hadn't done anything to break our bond. It's been a few hours since he turned Hunter and Athena took him off to the Elders. My dad finally just walked into the door to let us all know how things went down with the brothers, and how Brandon died.

"But how did he know where we were, and how did you know where to find him?" I cross my arms as I wait for his answer.

"He—*they*—were bonded to Hunter. The bond let them know where he was. I have no idea how he found out Hunter was helping us capture them. How did I know where he was, you ask? That dirty ass vampire had a scent that he couldn't hide anywhere. Once he escaped, we headed back into the underground. After we got here, we caught his scent and chased him. He'd already drawn his weapon and had it aimed toward you all by the time we found him. Luckily, Athena was there to flash you all away to somewhere else. I hate that Hunter was hit, but now that he's changed, he'll be much better off not being bonded to those assholes anymore." Once again, my dad loves to say it all without taking a breath.

He moves from where he was standing next to me over to where Austin is leaning against the bar, placing his hand on his shoulder.

"So, I hear you're now a sire, and on your first day as a vampire," he tells him.

"Yes sir, but I'm not sure if that is a good or bad thing," Austin replies with that damn smirk he always has. You would think he was being a smartass, but the smirk was a dead giveaway of being unsure of the answer he's given. It hadn't taken me long to figure that out.

"You'll do fine, Austin, I'm sure of it. Besides, you have us all here to help you. You're our family now, remember that. Hunter shall be also, once he has learned to control himself. You also have Athena and the Elders on your side. You're very lucky to have what many never have in their life as a vampire. I must shower and rest for a while now," my dad says as he excuses himself, going into my parents' bedroom.

Mom and I clean the blood from the floor using some super cleaner they use to remove blood stains. The moment you spray it on, the blood disappears. I suppose being a vampire this stuff comes in pretty handy. We spray the bloody towels with the cleaner as well and place them into the washer.

"Haley, grab your mate and come with me. It's time I show you two the secret surprise I've been preparing for you," my mom tells me as she starts the washer.

Leaving the lair, we take a left into the alleyway. After walking for maybe a hundred feet, we turn left into another alleyway, where my mother stops and turns to face a bright yellow door. She takes a key from her pocket and unlocks the door, opening it and standing to the side, looking at Austin and I as if we are supposed to do something.

"Are you going in or are you going to stand there and look at me as if I'm a crazy lady?" Mom asks, motioning for us to go inside.

"Why are we here, and why didn't you go in before us?" I ask, walking into what looks to be a lair. "Did you bring us to someone else's home, Mom?"

The walls are just as colorful as the bright yellow door that opened into the room. Sky blue, I think is what you would call it. The floor looks to be oak hardwood, and just like my parents' lair, there's a small kitchen with a bar, along with two doors on the other side of the room, which I'm sure are bedrooms. The living room is much smaller but cozy looking.

"No, Haley, this is yours. Yours and Austin's. Your father and I lived here before having you, and it's yours now. I had the walls and door painted brighter colors, so you wouldn't miss the outside world as much. You know, since Austin's now a vampire and will spend most of his time under-ground," Mom replies with a smile.

"How come you two have never spoken of this place? Have you owned it the whole time?" I ask, confusion washing over me.

"We sold it to a young couple and moved into the lair we own now, and that couple moved to another city a few months ago. We bought it in case your brother becomes full vampire on his birthday, so he would have a place when he was old enough. Once we found out you'd found your fated mate, we decided to let you and Austin stay here so you would be close by. Jonah will have to live with us a little longer, anyway." Mom chuckles.

"It's perfect, Mom. You guys didn't have to do this. We have my apartment. I could have made Austin sleeping quarters in my closet," I say, not realizing how dumb it must have sounded until the words were already out.

"Haley, I don't think sleeping in a closet is what you

really want for your mate. Now is it?" She asks, placing a hand midway up my back and walking with me to open the door into what I guess is our master bedroom.

The walls are painted a dark shade of purple, almost blue. The wood on the floor is a dark grey, as close as you can get to black. The linens look to be black satin, covering the four-post bed. To the right of the bed was a beautiful wooden box. The lid was open and lined with the same black silk that covers the bed. To the left of the bed was our master bathroom, covered in black marble.

"Wow, it's beautiful!" I glow.

"I hope you like it as well, Austin. We chose the coffin from a top of the line manufacturer. We wanted it to be as close to your bed and what you're used to as possible. We can always exchange it if you don't like it," she says, walking over with him to take a look inside.

"I was sleeping in a car, Mrs. Devile. I think anything will be better than that," he tells her, rubbing his hand around the outside of his sleeping box.

Yes, that's what I will call it because honestly, I hate the other word. Besides, why do the vampires of the underground still sleep in them? It's pitch black if you turn the lights off down here. I've never really become accustomed to the vampire's way of life, but it seems I have no choice now, since I'm to be the fated mate of one.

I walk behind him, just close enough he can feel my presence, and whisper into his ear. "I don't think I will allow you to leave the bed long enough to use this box."

The cute blush of pink that covers his face makes me laugh softly. I'm sure Mom knew I was up to no good, but it didn't matter to me. Austin on the other hand, looks as if he wishes he could jump into his sleeping box and close the lid as the pink shade of blush became more red.

"I'm glad you both like it. I was worried our color choices wouldn't be of your liking. Plus, we had to use vampire speed to have it done in only a few days."

"We love it, Mom. Right, Austin?" He just nods and smiles in agreement.

"I should be getting back now. I'll leave you two to get used to your new place," Mom says as we walk back into the living room.

"Goodnight, Mrs. Devile," Austin tells her as she closes the door behind her.

As much as I couldn't wait to be alone with Austin, shyness overcomes me. I feel like I'm looking at my first crush all over again as a nervous ball of butterflies starts to churn in my stomach. All the teasing and shit talking—all the waiting to touch him, kiss him, fuck him. Now here's my chance, and I stand here trembling, asking myself what I should do now.

Walking into the kitchen, I open the fridge, and to my surprise, I see my parents have it stocked for me. Bending to get a soda from the bottom shelf, I feel the heat of Austin moving up behind me. He places his hands on each of my hips and nudges himself against my ass. Passion fills my body, and the electricity I feel from him touching me is ten times stronger than any other time I've felt it.

I can only imagine how it's going to feel once we're skin to skin. Pushing back against him, I stand up straight and close the door, forgetting to even get my soda as I turn to face him. Damn, he seems to get better looking every time I look at him.

"Austin, you're being bad," I say with a smirk.

"You think I'm being bad? You should see what you've done to me," he replies as he reaches down to grab himself, putting his bulging pants on full display.

"Me? How did I do that, you were the one pushing up on me?" I ask him as I move closer, closing the space between us. If had to admit it, I was just as horny as he looked. Thank God that we don't have to worry about hard-ons as women. I snicker louder than I thought I had.

He looks so serious as he gazes at me. "Why is that funny, Haley?"

I just play as if I'm not still giggling on the inside. Who knew I would be so giggly around him when we were alone? *Get it together Haley, this is your mate and damn, he's fine as fuck. Mine,* I think to myself.

Last week I was single and not even looking for a boyfriend, and just enjoying life. Today, here I stand in my own kitchen with a mate—a *vampire* mate, nonetheless. A mate that any woman would give her left tit to have, and he's mine, all mine.

"Nothing's funny. I just giggled at the thought of you always getting hard so easily," I say as I sit on the couch.

"Oh, so easily huh? You think it just happens so easy? You're the only person who's ever made me feel this way, Haley. I get turned on just looking at you. Knowing you're my mate makes it even more of a turn on. I've controlled myself for about as long as I can now. Now that I've changed, I can make it complete. I can make you my mate. Let me take you, Haley. I want to leave my mark on you for the world to see. Let me make you my mate."

He's speaking, but the only thing I hear is my name and the word *mate* in one sentence. Little did he know that in my mind, I've already mated and claimed him. It's just a matter of physically doing so at this point. My panties are soaked and my body is tingling at the thought.

"*Make* me? I'm already your mate, Austin," I tell him as he walks to stand in front of me where I'm sitting on the couch. His bulge is only inches from my face, and heat radiates from him. This vampire is no cold dead soul. He is very much alive and hot, very hot.

Was it our connection, our fate—am I the only one who can feel the heat from him? Why do I even worry about that in this moment? No one else is ever going to get close enough to feel anything on this man, other than me. He reaches down to place his index finger under my chin, lifting my head up to look at him. Our eyes meet, and I lose all thought of anything else.

"You like what you see, Haley?" he asks, looking down at me with that fucking smirk. Did he even have to ask that question, could he not tell by the way I was staring? I reach to place my hand on his crotch.

"You mean this, Austin?" I sigh as I rub my hand onto his pant covered cock.

He grins. "Actually, I was talking about just me in general, but I'm okay with you liking that, too."

It felt amazing, rubbing him through his pants, but I'm ready for skin contact. I want to feel the energy that's built between us. Moving my hand from where I was rubbing him, I reach up to grab the button on his jeans. As I start to undo it, he pushes my hand away. Grabbing my wrist lightly, he pulls me up to come face to face with him.

"I get to taste you first," he says, leaning in to kiss me.

Our lips meet and it feels like I've been hit with a taser— but in a good way. A wave of electricity rushes through my veins yet again, only this time even stronger than before. He rubs his fingers up my arm and just the tingle alone almost makes me lose all control.

If a body could have an orgasm from a single touch, then that's what it feels like. Once he's reached the top of my arm, he rubs up my shoulder and onto my neck. Pushing my hair up, he wraps his hand behind my neck and pulls me into him. He plunges his tongue into my mouth, and I match his motion with mine. I think the vampire side of me is starting to show, because I want to bite his neck. Fuck, I even want to taste his blood, I want to claim him.

And I want him to claim me—all of me.

Chapter 29

AUSTIN

J ust days ago, I was freezing in my car and wondering where I was going to go with my life. No family, no one to turn to, no place to go. Working a job two days a week, only making enough money to keep me fed. Tonight, I stand with Haley in our beautiful lair, as a vampire making out with my mate. This is where I'm meant to be, where I am supposed to be. The life that fate has chosen for me.

It's hard to keep our fangs from clashing, but somehow, we've found our rhythm. Every nerve is my body is tingling and I can feel myself feeding off of her energy. I wrap my hand around her neck and pull her in closer to me, plunging my tongue deeper into her mouth.

I can only stand this for a few more minutes before I have to claim what's mine. I can tell she wants this as much as I do, I can sense it. I never thought it would be possible to sense someone's arousal. I really have a lot of fun things— and, I'm sure, not so fun things—to learn about being a vampire. But all I want to learn right now is every part of Haley's body.

Moving away, I grab her by the hand and lead her to the bedroom. "Haley, I want you, but I want to be sure this is what you want. I want to make you mine and claim you as my mate. Is this what you want? Me, your mate, here and now?" I ask her as I look her in her sparkling blue eyes.

"Yes, Austin. I've never been more certain of anything

else in my life. This is what I want and where I want to be. Besides, it's fated, remember? If it's meant to be then it shall be done. Claim me Austin, but I will be claiming you as well," she replies, gently kissing me as she pulls away and releases my hand, giggling while she prances into the bedroom.

Of course, I follow without any hesitation. My dick is raging in my pants. This is nothing like when I was human. It's thicker, harder, and—*wow*—maybe even a little longer. I think I'm going to like this part of being a vampire. Walking over to where she is standing next to the footboard, I pick her up and gently lay her down on the bed.

Reaching down, I find the button of her jeans, quickly releasing it and unzipping her pants. Grabbing them with my hands on each side, I slide them down her beautifully toned thighs, past her knees, over her ankles, and then throw them onto the floor, her panties following shortly behind.

I want to be much more aggressive, but first I want to please my mate, and the need to do so overrides what I want. I run my fingers up each side of her leg, around her folds, and just before I reach her clit, I start back down again. Once I reach her ankles, I lean down and put my tongue on her leg, licking my way back up. She whimpers and raises her ass off the bed when I reach her pussy. I make short passes over her clit, taking a moment to look up at her with a grin.

"You like that, mate?" Not giving her time to reply, I move down, slipping my tongue inside her.

Fuck, she tastes amazing! Slipping a finger inside her, I move my tongue to her clit. She moans my name, along with a few *oh my gawds* to follow. Her eyelids flutter as her eyes start to roll back, and she squeezes them tightly shut. Slowly, I lick my way up her body, with two fingers now inside her. Once I reach her breast, I open my mouth over her nipple and begin to suck it, moving my fingers faster as I push them in deeper. She reaches to grab my hair and I move up to whisper in her ear.

"You're so hot, Haley, and you taste amazing. Are you ready for me?" I ask as I let my fangs gently scrape down the back of her neck.

"So ready, Austin. Take me, I'm all yours."

That was all she had to say, or maybe all she *could* say. I move myself up, placing my throbbing cock against her opening. I teased her with the head, rubbing it on her clit, and nudging into her just enough to make her want more, as I lean down so my body is on top of hers.

The heat between us is almost unbearable, in an amazing kind of way. Our connection is like nothing I've ever felt before. It's a force pulling me into her, sending electric waves radiating throughout my body. I put my arm under her and pull her up from the bed a bit and grab her hair with the other hand just as I push myself into her.

Shit, she's so tight I have to stop at less than halfway in and let her adjust to my width, letting my head rest on her shoulder. Her vein is in full view and I can't control myself any longer.

The vampire is now who I am, and I have no control over my actions right now.

"Austin, just you touching my skin alone is about to make me lose my mind. Don't keep teasing me," she moans.

I pull out just enough to leave the head inside, then all the way out to run the head over her clit. I give it a few slaps and then lick up her neck, stopping to lightly suck on my way, and then I grab her chin and turn her to kiss me.

"You're mine, Haley, and I'm about to take what's mine," I tell her as I slam my full length into her pussy.

She bucks against me, trying to pull away, but not in pain. She's pulling away like it's too much all at once. I don't let her get away with that, though. I pull back and ram myself in harder this time, so hard I feel her wetness on my balls.

"Fuck me," she screams.

"Are you sure you can take it, Haley? I'm not going to hold anything back."

I pulled her hair back, bringing her neck into full view. The vein and her voice are now begging me to take them both.

"I can handle it. Claim me, Austin," she whimpers.

I slow my strokes as she relaxes, starting to match my movements.

"Can you feel the energy between us, Haley? Do you feel the force that's pulling us together?" I whisper to her as I nibble on her ear.

"It's amazing, Austin. The pain has become pleasure. I don't ever want it to stop," she replies, grabbing my hair this time and pulling me in to kiss her.

I pull out just long enough to look her in the eyes, showing her my fangs. Just before I slam into her again and then finally, *I claim my mate*. My fangs push into her tender neck and the amazing copper taste that hits my tongue sends me over the edge.

I begin sucking the blood in pure ecstasy. I feel her clamping onto my cock harder as she moans through an orgasm. I've waited for this and the pressure that's built eases from my body as I release myself inside her.

She's sated beneath me now, and I remove my fangs from her neck and lick the remaining blood clean. I felt myself go limp inside her before I pull out and roll over onto my back.

Looking up at the ceiling, I can feel her life force running through my veins. My soul hasn't left me, as I am just now finding it. The pull between us is stronger and just lying next her I can feel her energy surrounding me. I don't have to touch her to feel her any longer.

I clear my throat and find the words to speak.

"Haley, you're fucking amazing. Fate could not have given me a more beautiful mate. Will you marry me under the light of the blood moon?" I ask her when she finally looks like she's able to speak again.

"You're the amazing one, Austin. And yes, I will marry you. You did just claim me after all, so you're stuck with me anyway. I suppose I can wait a few more days to claim what's mine as well," she says with a little grin.

"You can claim me, but I'm already yours, Haley. *Always and forever.*"

The End... *for now.*

About Livell James

Livell is a lover of all things inspiring and a multitude of art forms.

I have told stories with photography for many years and decided to put pen to paper for the stories I feel can only be told with my words. My debut story in a planned series is paranormal romance co-written by fellow Author Chelsea Handcock. When I am not writing or taking photos, I enjoy spending time with my wife and checking items off my bucket list.

facebook.com/livelljames

instagram.com/authorlivelljames

bookbub.com/authors/livell-james

More Books by
Livell James

The Dirt Road Series

Cowritten with Chelsea Handcock

Down the Dirt Road

Dirt Road Redemption